Show Me Your Teeth

Amy Marsden

by Amy Marsden

VAMPIRES
We're All Monsters Here
Show Me Your Teeth

SURVIVORS duology
Survivors
The Safe Zone

Copyright © 2024 by Amy Marsden

All rights reserved.

No part of this book may be reproduced in any form or by any electronic or mechanical means including information about storage and retrieval systems, without permission in writing from the author.

This book is a work of fiction. Names, characters, places, and incidents are either products of the author's imagination or are used fictitiously. Any resemblance to actual persons, living or dead, events, or locales is entirely coincidental.

Content warnings: sex, blood, violence, death

This book is written in British English.

To my wife.
Now and always.
Thank you for reading this even more than I have.

1

I contemplated tearing the man's throat out, but as I was in the middle of a crowded street in broad daylight, I ultimately decided against it. A pity, really. Entitled manbabies deserved my fangs as far as I was concerned. However, not only would blood ruin my lovely new coat that swished around my knees and kept the October chill at bay, but the existence of vampires would be revealed to the world, and nobody wanted that.

Alas, the bastard continued to live another day. Besides, if I killed every fool who pissed me off, I'd leave a pile of bodies to rival Everest.

Michaela chuckled beside me. "You look like you've stepped in dog shit."

I rolled my eyes at her as we moved on from the screaming man, who yelled profanity at some poor slip of a woman who had apparently almost 'knocked him flying'. What an overreaction. He was at least double her weight. "Stepping in dog shit would be preferable to listening to him berate that woman for no good reason."

Seeing some arsehole make a scene had soured my already bad mood further. Michaela and I had gotten into an argument last night. *Were all students so stubborn?* I was her mentor, I knew best, yet she fought against my advice and wisdom more and more.

Well, that wasn't entirely true. She fought me on one specific thing, but it was pretty damn important, and I was sick of trying to drill it into her. I understood, of course. She was a grown women who knew her mind and what she wanted, and she had been doing well by herself. Up to a point, anyway. We'd been in Ireland for little over a year and staying in one place was antithesis to my personality, especially considering the amount of blood Michaela drank. I suspected hunters would soon be on our tail. Michaela, on the other hand, liked Ireland, Dublin in particular, and pushed back against me every time I suggested leaving, to the point we had a full-blown argument about it. Shouting, screaming, the works.

We apologised to each other that morning and she took me shopping—hence the new coat—but I continued to wear petulance like a second skin, and I did *not* like it. There were few emotions more useless than sulking, and I hadn't been this sullen in a good long while. Despite apologising, she hadn't changed her mind. Why wouldn't she *listen* to me? The whole mentoring thing was far more difficult than I had anticipated.

And, to add insult to injury, the rumblings of hunger disturbed my stomach, like distant thunder at the edge of hearing. It had only been two months since I'd last fed, but the human trafficking ring I'd uncovered—and by uncovered I meant stumbled upon wholly by accident after following a drunken idiot back to his home—had been small and inept and obviously not enough. It had been good to kill them, though. Feeding on the worst of humanity never failed to fill me with a vicious delight. But I wanted to *leave*, not research who to kill next. My growing hunger would force us to make a decision sooner rather than later and I sincerely hoped Michaela came round to my way of thinking before it got to that point.

We needed to leave. We'd been in Dublin way too long, Michaela's body count was way too high, and there had been no indication whatsoever of Saira finding me.

My mood dipped lower, which was ridiculous. I'd only known her for a few days, and she was a *hunter*, for crying out loud. I had no business getting upset that she hadn't tracked me down. It was a good thing. It meant all my precautions worked. As long as I continued evading hunters, I could live an even longer life yet.

"Hey, what about this? I bet it would look beautiful on you. Really bring out your eyes."

Michaela dragged me over to the window of a jewellery shop, pointing at a necklace. Granted, it was gorgeous, but not even emeralds could pull me out of my head. "Look, thanks for the coat, but I'm going to go home. Are you coming, or will I see you later?"

Michaela sighed. "I get that you're upset, but I spent six years in one place with the Beyer Corporation, feeding even more often than I do now. I don't think we need to be panicking just yet."

"Okay, one, New York City is a *lot* bigger than Dublin. Two, hunters still found you anyway," I snapped, not bothering to control my irritation. "You need to—"

"Can we not do this here?" Michaela cut me off, annoyance making her Canadian accent even more pronounced. A couple of people passing by shot us glances.

"Fine. I'll see you later."

I strode away without another word or backwards glance, too angry to worry about her. If she got hungry and killed some poor sap, that was on her, not me. Honestly, vampires who turned others had astronomical levels of patience. *This is why I was never interested, for over five centuries.* I cursed the day I found her and decided to help. I could've been somewhere warm at that moment, planning my next feed in the lap of luxury instead of cold, rainy Dublin. Maybe I could have still been in touch with Saira, as my identity probably wouldn't have been revealed. I imagined it, only myself to look after, no burde—

I cut off that line of thinking. It was the anger talking. I would never have left Michaela there to fend for herself; yes, I could be a pretty selfish person, but vampires looked out for each other. An unspoken rule we all followed. And Michaela had grown into a good friend. I wouldn't be disrespectful by thinking ill of her.

Instead of going back to the house Michaela and I rented with the money I had stashed away in numerous accounts, I turned deeper into the city, hunting for an Internet café. Which, by the way, were becoming more and more scarce as the decades flashed by. I could have gone to a library, but they required you to join, and the smaller my digital footprint, the better. I had various encrypted emails I checked every now and then—it was how my friends and I kept in touch in the modern world—and liked the anonymity of not owning a computer. Less chance I could be traced by savvy hunters. I didn't fully understand all the encryptions and security on the emails, despite taking a couple of computer science courses, but Lilli, a good friend I'd met in Germany after the First World War, was a bit of a savant when it came to technology and assured me it was safe.

It took me an hour of wandering around to find an Internet café. There were only three people inside, all men, and I felt their stares like physical blows. Ugh, they didn't even make an attempt at subtlety. Male attention was tedious at best, deadly at worst, and I ignored them as I sat down and started up a monitor.

I would never tell Lilli, but I had the same password for all my email addresses. In my defence, it was a random selection of letters and numbers, some upper case and some lower case, that I didn't think your average hunter could guess. Still, Lilli would've *definitely* been pissed if she found out, and would yell at me in a tangle of German and English I would have trouble following.

After another hour of catching up with correspondence, I noticed an email from Colette. It wasn't unusual—we messaged each other regularly—but what caught my eye was that she was in *Dublin*. I quickly scrolled back through our previous messages, but she'd made no mention of Ireland at all. It had been almost eighty years since I'd last seen her in person—the longest we'd ever gone without seeing one another since we'd met. My stomach flipped as a grin spread over my face. It would be *so* good to see her again. Not only would it be wonderful to catch up with someone I loved, but she'd turned two vampires in the past, and I could use some of her expertise. I smiled as I pictured her face when I told her I was mentoring someone. She'd probably keel over in shock.

I responded with a message of my own, saying I'd love to meet up as soon as possible. Maybe she'd help me forget about Saira, for a few hours at least. I logged out with a sigh. I wasn't sure. Colette and I loved each other deeply, and somehow always made our way back into one other's arms. That being said, if she was interested in someone, or vice versa, we respected that and kept our distance. Unless, of course, the other woman liked us both. Polygamy wasn't for everyone, however; I could count on one hand the number of throuples we'd been in.

The last time we'd seen each other, nothing sexual had happened. Not only were we busy killing nazi's, but she had been hung up on a woman and only had eyes for her. Maybe after eighty years, however...

the thought trailed off. I was the one hung up on a woman this time. Don't get me wrong, I hadn't been celibate this past year, but those had been meaningless one-night stands with strangers. I didn't think I could sleep with someone I'd known and loved for centuries whilst Saira clung to the corners of my mind.

I stood and stretched. Night encroached, a sudden sweep of shadows shoving the light away, and my latest book was waiting for me at home. As soon as Colette got back to me, I'd meet up with her and get some advice, then plan my next moves.

Hunger stirred, faint and hazy, but stronger than a few hours ago. I ignored it as best I could.

2

To my surprise, another email from Colette sat in my inbox the very next day. I'd gone back to the Internet café on a whim, my burgeoning hunger kicking me into research mode. That part of the feeding process could be either tedious or exciting, depending on my mood, but I did always enjoy investigating which shitty people I had the best chance of murdering. I also hoped for a quick reply from Colette, although the rational part of me hadn't expected one. I checked my emails every few weeks or so; Colette checked hers every two or even three months. Maybe she'd still been catching up on the backlog she no doubt had, and my email had pinged at the top.

So, I found myself, the day after *that*, seated in the café at the National Botanical Gardens, waiting for my long-time *companion*—a running joke between us, see gal pals in modern speak.

We spotted each other at the same time. She'd styled her mahogany hair differently to what I remembered, shaved at the sides with the longer top falling loose over her shoulders, but it still suited her. Honestly, there weren't many looks Colette couldn't pull off. Her thick maroon hoodie swamped her lithe frame, just the way she liked, and it looked far more comfortable than my own cream jumper. The last time I'd seen her, her hair had been short all over and styled in a masculine cut. For as long as I'd known her, Colette had experimented with gender presentation; no easy feat a few decades ago, never mind in the centuries since we'd met. In fact, I recalled her wearing trousers the first time I laid eyes on her. Seeing a woman wear what she wanted, with no care as to the consequences, was what initially drew me to her. I'd never seen someone look so *free*. Don't get me wrong, I myself had worn 'male' clothing before, but I'd never seen a woman fit it so well. I was instantly taken with her. Thankfully, in the modern world, gender didn't hold clothing in the same chokehold as it once had.

When I questioned her about her attire, she'd told me Jeanne d'Arc was an inspiration and proceeded to list all the negative things the English had done to the French. I'd thought she hated me because of the country I'd been born in three centuries prior, but after her passionate speech she'd laughed—a wild, free sound I'd immediately wanted to hear again—linked my arm and took me on the kind of tour of Paris only a local would know.

She gave me a small wave and smiled in that easy way of hers, and a powerful bolt of nostalgia hit me square in the chest, my breath leaving my lungs in a rush. I made it a point then to make an effort to meet up with her and my other friends more often than I already did. A few times a decade wasn't enough. *Curse* hunters for making me so skittish. Maybe Michaela's nonchalance was rubbing off on me. I didn't know if that was a good thing or not.

Shoving myself to my feet, I grabbed Colette and pulled her into a tight embrace, the smell of roses winding up my nose. That was new. But then, Colette loved trying different perfumes and aftershaves. I'd never understood the appeal; as long as I smelled clean and fresh, I was happy. Humans often stank so strongly of a particular scent it was sometimes difficult to catch their blood underneath it all.

"Anna, it's *so good* to see you after all this time." Her accent held more French than I remembered, perhaps she'd been back recently? "This is Graciela Garcia, who goes by Gracie, a new friend who wanted to meet you and see the Botanical Gardens."

I blinked at Gracie, noticing her for the first time as she stepped forward with a shy wave and a ducked head. She was a vampire—I recognised our almost unnatural beauty right away, her dark hair perfectly curled, her tanned skin perfectly flawless—but she lacked the confidence longevity gave us, even dressed in stylish black jeans and a jade shirt that brought out the green in her hazel eyes. Was she a new one Colette had turned? That would be a great way for me to bring up Michaela.

"It's so good to see you too. And nice to meet you as well, Gracie," I said, equal parts happy to meet more of my kind and irritated I couldn't catch up with Colette alone.

"I'll get us some waters," Gracie mumbled before dashing off into the crowd. Water was a good cover for us in cafés and restaurants—it was the only thing besides blood we could consume without feeling sick.

I raised an eyebrow at Colette who, despite not seeing me for decades, still knew how to read my expressions.

She rolled her eyes. "It's not like that. Gracie is lovely, and is bisexual, but she's a little too... how do I put it. She's too wet around the ears for me. You know I like women with more drive and experience." She waggled her eyebrows, and I chuckled. Pursuing women with *drive* and *experience* had landed Colette in trouble more times than I could remember.

I sat back down while Colette settled into to seat opposite me. My eyes wandered over her, drinking her in after so long apart. My usual feeling of desire for her was a little muted, though. I sighed internally, annoyed at myself for getting so hung up over a damn *hunter* I hadn't even seen in over a year. Perhaps getting involved with Colette again would help me get past Saira, but I didn't want to use her that way. I had far too much respect for her.

"Is Gracie newborn?" I asked, pushing aside my spiralling thoughts. *Focus on the here and now. Focus on getting reacquainted after not seeing each other for ages.*

Colette shrugged one shoulder. "Yes, but I didn't turn her. She says she's exactly fifty, turned thirty years ago. I've known her for several months and she's just as shy now as when we first met." Colette leaned forward, a familiar spark dancing in her ocean eyes. I knew instantly that she'd found a new hobby. It was good for us to keep learning new things. It helped stave off the stagnation of immortality.

"I've taken an interest in botany and found myself a group of like-minded people to study with," Colette said, eagerness twisting her lips into a smile. "There are five of us. Gracie always says she prefers plants to people, and I'm beginning to see why. I can't believe I've never taken an interest before now. You were right, it's so *interesting*. It's been both good and bad, so far. Good in that we're all pretty much at the same level, apart from William, who's teaching us, and bad in that they're all young. We have to move a lot. William is the oldest at a hundred and ninety-five."

Worry curled through me like fog, tendrils wrapping around my chest and squeezing my lungs. A hundred and ninety-five wasn't old at all. And if he was the oldest... "You need to be careful."

"I know, I know." Colette didn't seem to share my concern. She always was more blasé about hunters than me. Maybe *I* was the one in the wrong, always uptight about those genocidal maniacs. Colette was still alive after all, and she was only five years younger than me. But no. After everything I'd seen, after all the times hunters had caught up with my friends, staying still wasn't in my bones. I needed to *move*.

"It's why we're in Dublin, actually," Colette continued, a frown marring her forehead.

"What is?" The fog thickened, threatening to strangle me. Hunters hadn't caught Colette's scent, had they? I'd lost so many people to them; I *couldn't* lose her too.

Gracie came back at that moment, three glasses of water in her hands. I accepted mine with a quick smile and put it on the table in front of me, too focused on Colette to keep up the pretence of being human.

"Are you interested in botany, Anna?" The heavily Spanish accented voice was quiet, and when I made eye contact with her, Gracie looked down.

I swallowed my impatience. "I used to be, about a hundred and fifty years ago," I said, keeping my tone conversational. Gracie seemed sweet, and it wouldn't do to take my frustration out on her. Colette could keep her secrets a little while longer. "I'm actually surprised Colette is so interested now, since she avoided my every effort to include her back then." I gave her a stern look, but my smile took the sting out of it.

Colette let out her beautiful, wild laugh. "If I remember correctly, I became fascinated by economics due to the Panic. I had no time for flowers with all that going on."

"The Panic?" Gracie looked so confused. It was cute. She really was young.

"The Panic of 1873." I shook of my head. "It was a global depression. Not *fascinating* at all."

"I beg to differ," Colette said, a challenge in her eyes. She always did love debates. "The Vienna Stock Exchange crashed—"

"*Please* don't make me listen to it all again," I groaned, prompting another laugh from Colette and a small smile from Gracie. Despite living for over five hundred years and having more knowledge on the subject than most people, economics always managed to bore me to tears. "Besides, didn't it start in Europe in Germany, after they beat France in the Franco-Prussian War?"

That got a huff out of Colette, which never failed to amuse me. I'd long since let go of any ties to my birth country, but Colette, for reasons that continued to baffle me, hadn't been able to do the same with France.

"Economics are far more interesting than fish," Colette sniped back, her fond eye roll bringing a smile to my face.

"Fish?" Gracie asked, confused.

"I studied marine biology about twelve years ago," I said affectionately. It was the last time I'd studied a subject at university, and I had nothing but good memories from that period of my life. "There was a little more to it than just looking at 'fish'." I'd travelled up and down the west coast of North America for six years putting that degree to good use. I'd only moved to the east coast after I grew a little too paranoid about being in the same general area for so long. Hunters really did ruin everything.

"We're getting side tracked," I said, switching the subject back to what I wanted to talk about. "Why are you here? What happened?"

Colette let out a long sigh, her eyes darting to Gracie, who stared into her glass of water like it held the secrets to the universe. "I said everyone I'm with is young." I knew what she was saying. Four young vampires traveling together for an extended period of time would leave enough bodies to attract even the least experienced hunter, even with

Colette lending her expertise. Yes, the initial, overwhelming bloodlust began to die down after the first fifty years or so, but that didn't mean it vanished. A vampire who was a hundred, hundred and fifty, even two hundred sometimes still consumed a ridiculous amount of blood.

"Hunters picked up our scent in the US," Colette continued. I jolted in my seat; she'd been in the US? Not for long, surely? Had she been there when I'd been running my Beyer scam? "I convinced them we needed to leave the continent, and William asked if we could come here." She shrugged. "It's where he was born, and I guess he was feeling a little homesick."

Brushing aside the familiarities with mine and Michaela's situation, I leaned forward, careful not to knock my still full glass. None of us had touched our water. "Are you sure they didn't follow you? I mean it, Colette. You better have been thorough. We've lost too many people; I'll be damned before I lose you too."

The intensity in my voice drained the nonchalance from her face. "It's why we moved continents, not just countries. You know hunters are terrible at sharing information with other guilds, and I thought it would be even worse if we put an ocean between us. I would have preferred we move to a non-English speaking country, like back to Spain for Gracie, or China for Zhang Mei, so maybe any information they *do* share might get lost in translation, but ultimately, I didn't see anything wrong with Ireland."

They should have moved to a country none of them had any ties to, but it was done now. I slouched back in my chair. "How long have you been here?"

"Almost a month, right?" Colette looked to Gracie. I couldn't decide if it was an attempt to bring the other women into the conversation or if Colette was genuinely asking for confirmation.

"Yes," Gracie said in that quiet way of hers. "Three weeks and three days."

"Three weeks and three days," Colette parroted. "And no sign of any hunters." Her tone said that should be the end of it, nothing to concern myself about, but I was always going to worry.

Still, I let it go. Colette knew what she was doing, and while fear for her would always simmer below the surface, I trusted her to do the right thing if hunters found them.

"I have some news of my own," I said, twirling my glass of water on the table. I'd been vehemently against turning anyone or taking a young vampire under my wing for so long that it was almost embarrassing to say I had now. I inwardly scoffed. I needed to get over myself. People changed over time. If anyone understood that it would be us, who'd seen more change than all of humanity put together.

Colette cocked her head to the side, eyebrows raised in a question. Gracie looked on, polite curiosity twinkling in her eyes. "I've started mentoring a young vampire." Colette's raised eyebrows looked in danger of disappearing into her hairline, and I had to suppress the urge to giggle like an idiot. "Her name is Michaela. We met in the US…" I gave an abridged version of my time in America, realising all over again how close hunters had come to killing me. Goosebumps prickled along my skin. I *never* wanted to get that close to hunters ever again.

Well. With the exception of one hunter in particular.

I left Saira out of my retelling. It was silly, I know, but she was the highlight of that weekend and I wanted to keep her all to myself.

"Shit, Anna," Colette said, her eyebrows lowered in consternation. "You could have died. When you mentioned a '*brush with hunters*' in your emails, you didn't make it sound half as serious as it was. It makes sense now why you called off your five hundred and fortieth birthday celebrations; you were running from hunters. If I'd known all that I would've dropped everything and come to you sooner."

I waved her off. "It's fine—"

"It's *not* fine." She stood and pulled me to my feet, wrapping me in a bone-crushing embrace. I buried my face into her neck and let out a shaky breath as roses engulfed me. Despite it happening over a year ago, it hit me then that I could've never seen her again. I clung to her as tightly as she did me, only letting go when I felt her hold slacken.

"Don't do it again," she admonished, pointing a finger at me as we returned to our seats.

A breathy laugh escaped my lips. "I don't plan to."

Conversation moved to lighter topics, like we both needed to forget, for a little while at least, the threat hunters posed. Instead, we talked about what we'd both been up to these last few decades, Gracie's life and turning—which she readily volunteered, her turning not traumatic at all, unlike mine and Colette's and so many others—and what they'd learned studying botany so far. A lovely warmth settled in my chest, and before I knew it hours had passed.

I was rudely awoken from the happy cocoon the three of us were wrapped in by a plate of food being dropped onto the table with a clatter, followed by a body lowering itself onto the chair next to me. I glared at the offending food, the smell of cheap pizza almost overwhelming the smell of the person who had invited themselves to sit with us.

Almost, but not quite.

Her scent lit my every nerve alight, even after a year. The subtle sweetness of apricots hit me like a brick to the face, complimenting the intoxicating smell of her blood, and I could only stare at her smooth brown skin, her dark hair tied back in a loose bun, her pursed lips, her strong jaw, her narrowed eyes as they darted between the three of us.

"Hey, Anna. You look like you've seen a ghost. I don't look that bad, do I?"

Her American accent swirled around my ears, and all I could do was blink at her.

Saira.

What the fuck?

3

"It's been a long time. How are you?" Saira's voice sounded equal parts soft and rough, like seeing me had knocked her just as off-balance as it had me, but she'd tried to mask it. I felt winded, the mere sight of her sucker punching me right in the gut.

I was staring, mute, but I couldn't seem to do anything else. I'd resigned myself to never seeing her again, to her being nothing more than a strangely intense weekend fling I still needed to get over, yet there she was, pulling me right back into her orbit.

She looked great. Her face was a touch thinner, like she'd dedicated time to working out and had added muscle to her already lean frame. Her eyes were just as sharp as I remembered. I got the distinct feeling she was cataloguing everything, from Gracie's shyness to Colette's curiosity to the untouched waters in front of us all.

She was a little older, a little more sure of herself. I saw it in the relaxed way she slouched in her chair, her casual blue jeans and white jumper concealing a deadliness underneath. She held herself like she was in control of the situation despite being one hunter at a table of three vampires. Competence looked good on her. But then, she'd always been talented. She'd played her role in the Beyer corporation to perfection. She'd gotten the drop on Michaela, and she could have shot me had she known what I was at the time. Yeah, she was amazing. And that wasn't just my crush talking.

I'd been silently enraptured for too long. Catching Colette's smirk out of the corner of my eye, I realised my error right as she opened her mouth.

"Since all forms of polite etiquette seem to have fled Anna's mind, I'll have to introduce myself," Colette said, holding out a hand for Saira to shake. "I'm Colette. Anna's oldest and longest suffering friend."

"Is that so?" Saira shook her hand, an odd smile on her face. Another thought hit me then, another brick to the face. I felt as discombobulated as if I'd actually been hit with one. Saira was from the US. Colette and her new friends had just fled the US. *She's not hunting them... is she?* I'd never heard of hunters from one country following vampires to another. Had the protocol changed? Communication between guilds had always been mediocre at best. Were they finally getting their act together? Those horrifying thoughts were cut short by the sharpness of Saira's gaze on Colette. "I bet you have some stories to tell."

Colette laughed, putting on her winning smile as her eyes drank Saira up. "You have no idea."

Time to nip *that* in the bud. Although the thought of the three of us together—no. It wasn't the time or place to go there. Besides, I didn't know if Saira would like that. With a mental shake of my head to dislodge *those* thoughts, I turned my mind back to the present. What was the best play? Exposing her for a hunter would likely get her killed. Keeping quiet and informing Colette and Gracie later was the better option. They needed to leave as soon as possible.

"I'm Gracie."

Gracie's voice held a peculiar note. A glance over showed her eyes pinned on Saira like she was the most fascinating person in the room. Saira seemed unaffected by the weight of that gaze. A hot poker of jealousy stabbed my chest before I recognised the type of hunger in Gracie's eyes. I'd seen it in Michaela often enough to understand the danger. Gracie was young. Young vampires fed like it was going out of fashion. A sharper, more frantic feeling landed next to the jealousy.

No one touched Saira. Not on my watch.

"Saira."

I was suddenly glad I'd omitted her earlier. Colette wouldn't have made a scene, and I didn't think Gracie would have either, but I had only just met her. I didn't know how she'd react if she knew she sat across from a hunter.

I still hadn't said anything. What was wrong with me? Over five hundred years old, acting like a nervous teenager. *What a disgrace.*

Gracie's stomach rumbled.

Saira froze for the briefest of seconds. I would've missed it had I not been watching her so closely. She raised an amused eyebrow to cover her little slip. The others didn't seem to have noticed anything.

"Hungry? Want a slice?" She held up some pizza, and it was almost funny to watch Gracie recoil in disgust. "Don't like pizza, huh. That sucks." Saira took a massive bite out of the slice, and I was both impressed and repulsed by how much she shoved into her mouth.

I found my voice at last. "Saira, darling, it's been too long. What brings you to Ireland? I thought you couldn't travel."

She took her time chewing. I reached for my glass and downed half the contents. Water tasted of nothing to my blood loving tastebuds, but it was nice to wet my dry lips. I caught Colette's narrowed gaze; guzzling the water had tipped her off that something wasn't right.

Good. The sooner she left, the better. We could continue catching up later.

Saira finally finished her bite of pizza. The smell of which was openly attacking my nostrils, by the way. I took a breath through my mouth instead, but that felt like I was eating it. I couldn't win.

"A new job opportunity came up," Saira finally answered, "and I jumped at the chance. You know how much I've always wanted to travel."

"That's wonderful. I'm happy for you." Despite how stilted my sentences were, I *was* genuinely happy she was seeing some of the world. Her desire to travel had been one of the sincerest things about her. The silly urge to show her the world rose within me again, even after so long, a balloon that eluded all attempts at popping. My feelings were playing with fire and didn't seem to care about getting burnt.

"I haven't been here long, but it's *amazing*," Saira gushed. A warm smile settled on my face; this was Saira the person, real and honest, not Saira the hunter, who I didn't really want to see. "It's so different," she continued. "The money is colourful, which is random, I know, but I love it. Everything is on a smaller scale, like the cars and roads. And I really like that the tax is incorporated into the price here. I never knew anything different, but now that I do, I don't understand why we don't do it in the US."

"Is this your first time outside of the US?" Colette asked, her tone guarded. I saw the gears turning behind her eyes.

"Yes." Saira nodded. "What about you? You don't have an Irish accent. What is that... French?"

Colette hummed. "What brought you to Ire—"

She didn't finish the question. Saira threw her arm up, an accusatory finger pointed right at Gracie. The hairs on the back of my neck stood on end. "Don't even think about it." Danger dripped from

Saira's voice, and my stomach absolutely did *not* tighten with arousal at the sound. No way. How messed up would that be?

I looked at Gracie, who's hands were flat on the table like she'd been about to push herself to her feet. She hadn't been about to dive on Saira, had she? In the middle of a very public, very crowded café? Incredulousness made my heart thud against my ribs. I would have thought, after thirty years, Gracie had slightly more control than that.

"I know vampires have a certain flavour of arrogance to them," Saira growled, "but surely you weren't about to attack me right here, in this crowded room." She picked up a backpack I hadn't even noticed and reached inside, briefly pulling out a tranquiliser gun before concealing it once more. "Besides, you'd have a dart in you before you got out of your chair."

I squeezed my eyes shut. *Great. Just great.* There went my idea of quietly informing Colette and Gracie later. Now I was going to have to protect Saira. A *hunter*. What had my life come to?

"A fucking hunter, Anna?" Colette hissed, her back ramrod straight. "Seriously?"

Saira waved a dismissive hand. "Anna and I were a one-time thing before we knew the truth about each other. I'm not here for her. I'm here for you two, and your little band of botanists."

I didn't hear the rest of what she said because... okay. The way she'd downplayed our connection hurt. Way more than it should have. She was right, after all, and probably trivialising us for protection, but the sting made my blood roar in my ears, and my world narrowed to that point of pain. How fucking sad was I? Anger rose in response to the shame. I clenched my jaw and forced my way back into the conversation.

"Okay," I said, my voice cool and collected, no sign of my internal conflict. I waved a hand between Colette and Gracie. "It's time for you two to leave. We'll catch up properly at a later date. And you," I pointed a finger at Gracie, not unlike what Saira had done, "learn to control yourself better."

"They aren't going any—"

"Yes, they are." I cut Saira off, raising a calm eyebrow as she glared at me. "We are long overdue a chat, don't you think?"

We held eye contact for a beat, then another, and another. I couldn't read any expression in those swirling brown eyes of hers, and it reminded me how good of an actress she was. I'd never suspected she was anything other than Beyer's secretary for *months*. How much of her did I really know?

The thought cooled my attraction. She was a hunter, and I was a vampire. It wouldn't do to forget that.

Colette got up without a word, pulling Gracie to her feet as well. She hesitated, her eyes bouncing between me and Saira, silently asking if I was going to be all right. I nodded. Saira wouldn't hurt me. It was something we'd never explicitly talked about, but the truth of it sang in my bones. She wouldn't hurt me, and I wouldn't hurt her. A problem for both of us.

Saira watched them go while I watched Saira. Her lips were pursed, and a small frown pulled between her brows, but she didn't seem overly bothered her supposed prey were walking out the door.

A sensation like cold water dripped down my back. "Why aren't you chasing them?"

She turned in her seat until she fully faced me, a shrug pulling her shoulders up. "Other hunters are tailing them now. We need to find where they're staying, so we can get all of them."

My body flashed hot, and I had a horrible feeling of falling. "This was all a set up. You've been tailing them for a while and came over here with the intention of revealing you're a hunter, so they would run back to the others." At her nod, another thought occurred to me. "What about me? You said you'd kill me if you saw me again. Should I expect a dart in my back any second now?" My back began to itch, like someone had pressed a phantom weapon against me. I resisted the urge to glance around the bustling room.

For the first time since Saira sat down, her relaxed, capable façade cracked. Her tongue darted out to wet her lower lip, and her eyes flickered around my face before looking away. "No. I told my team you're an informant who helped me track them down."

I could only stare at her again. I'd known, deep down, that this wholly inconvenient infatuation went both ways, but it stole my breath to hear her say it out loud.

"Stop grinning at me like that," she snapped, the tiniest uptick of her lips belying her harsh tone. I hadn't even realised I was smiling. I finally felt like I'd regained my equilibrium with her. We were on the same page. Well, as much as a hunter and a vampire could be, anyway.

"Just so you know, Colette is over five hundred years old, and has evaded many hunters tracking her." Even as I spoke, all lingering tension took leave of my body. I had every faith in Colette. She knew what she was doing. You didn't get to our age without learning some tricks. "She won't lead your team to the rest of them. You might want to go back to the drawing board, because you lost them the moment they walked out of this building."

Saira stared at me, her mouth hanging open. Her stunned expression didn't fit with either my words or her proficiency. What had I said that was so shocking? She had to know there was a possibility they'd slip away.

"How old?"

The words were whispery, fragile things, like she'd just found out something she thought she knew as undeniable truth was, in fact, incorrect. The urge to tread carefully made my tongue sluggish in my mouth.

"She's five hundred and thirty-six, to be exact," I said slowly. I didn't know what the issue was and didn't want to upset her more.

Her throat bobbed as she swallowed. She blew out a breath, followed by a silent laugh that shook her shoulders. What was going on? Hunters knew vampires were essentially immortal. None of this was knew information. I was *so* confused.

"How old are you?" she asked suddenly, pinning me with an intensity that, in any other situation or place, would have had me shedding my clothes and pulling her onto me.

"I'm five hundred and forty-one. My birthday is in August, if you ever wish to send me a gift."

My admittedly rather feeble attempt at levity was lost on her as she blinked at me, her expression still stunned. I knew she was thirty. I knew her birthday was the third of December. If her fake Beyer employee information was correct, at least.

"Damn, you're old."

I couldn't help myself. Laughter erupted out of me, loud enough that people turned to look, but I didn't care. I hadn't been expecting her to say that, and the surprise tickled me more than was warranted.

"Rude," I said once I'd calmed down. "Don't you know never to comment on a lady's age?"

"My apologies," Saira said in a, quite frankly, appalling imitation of my accent. "I must have missed that etiquette lesson."

Her hand lay on the table next to her forgotten pizza, and I reached out and patted it. "Don't worry, there's still time for you to learn. Don't give up hope."

Warmth seeped from her to me, the air around us growing charged as I left my hand over hers. Her gaze lifted to meet mine, heavy-lidded, and I knew she felt it too. "How did you find me," I asked, my words soft, careful not to break the bubble we were in. My fingers traced the back of her hand. "Were you even looking for me, or was us seeing each other again a happy accident?"

She kept her eyes on mine, brown meeting green, a forest of secrets between us. "I *was* looking for you," she said, just as quietly. "But it's been slow. That retreat ruined my reputation, Anna. Taryn, the other hunter who survived, she told our superiors I'd cut a deal with a vampire. I've had to work my ass off this past year to scrape back the tiniest amount of respect. Looking for you in the middle of all of that was... unofficial.

"I found no trace of you besides your apartment in New York," she continued, a sarcastic note entering her tone. "Well done. You certainly know how to cover your tracks."

"So... how are you here?"

"I was given a team very recently. I guess I've proved myself enough to be trusted again." I didn't want to know what 'proving herself' meant. I didn't want to know how many of my kind she'd killed. Burying my head in the sand had never been more appealing.

"I stopped tracking you and started tracking Michaela," she continued. "I was working with *a lot* of assumptions. Given the lengths you went to for her, I assumed you'd still be travelling together. I assumed you'd go to Canada but found nothing. I assume Michaela Finn isn't her real name?" The question was rhetorical, and I remained quiet as she continued talking.

"Her ties to Ireland were flimsy at best, a couple of old social media posts about her having family from here, but when the vamps my team were hunting up and left for Ireland, I figured it was worth a shot. If it was a dead end, we still get those vamps. Tracking vampires between countries isn't really protocol—" *I knew it!* "—but it has been done before, so there was precedent. I pushed hard to come here. I guess they think I'm still pushing hard to prove myself, so they didn't suspect ulterior motives. Seeing you again was a bonus." She leaned back in her chair, making no move to dislodge my hand. "I honestly didn't expect to find you. Now that I have... I don't know what to do." She gave a bitter laugh, her gaze falling away and landing on our hands. She flipped them over and started drawing patterns on my palm. It tickled, but I held still.

"You won't get '*those vamps*', as you put it," I sighed, the urge to scratch my hand almost overwhelming.

"No?" she quirked an eyebrow. "And why is that?"

"Young vampires attract you hunters like lodestones, yes, but Colette is experienced. She'll get them away."

"You seem so sure."

"I am. She's endured worse situations."

Saira's fingers stilled, her expression turning almost wistful. "I can see that. Over five hundred years old. The places you've seen, the things you've lived through. It's crazy to think about."

"Pick an historical event and I'll tell you if I was there and what it was like." The enthusiasm in my voice should have been embarrassing, but I just wanted to keep chatting to her.

She didn't pick an historical event. Her gaze sharpened, and I wondered what I'd said to set alarm bells ringing her in head.

She didn't keep me in suspense for long. "You said *young* vampires. And back at that retreat, you were surrounded by blood but didn't look twice at it. So, what, the older a vamp gets, the more they can control their bloodlust?"

Reality sharply reasserted itself at her question. The last thing I wanted was to give hunters information about us they didn't know, so I held my tongue. Not that it mattered; my silence was confirmation enough. I cursed myself for being so careless. I needed to leave before I forgot more of myself around her and said something that handed every vampire over to hunters on a silver platter.

She seemed to sense our conversation was over. Reaching into her backpack, she pulled out a pen and grabbed my hand again before I could shove my fists into my pockets.

"Call me," she said. I looked at the number scribbled over my palm, a giddiness curling my lips upward. "Or text. That would be better, actually." She chuckled. "Who calls people these days?"

I gripped her hand and brought her knuckles to my lips, pressing down lightly. "Until next time."

She rolled her eyes at me, but the flush in her cheeks told me I'd hit the mark. "Get out of here." She shooed me away. "And even though I said you're an informant, keep an eye—"

"—out for anyone tailing me, yes," I finished for her. "I wasn't born yesterday." Throwing a smirk her way, I sauntered out of the café, her chuckle carrying me into the afternoon sunshine.

What a day.

4

The house Michaela and I rented was modest, semi-detached, and in a nice area. It wasn't the best place I'd ever lived, but it was a far cry from the worst, and I was happy to call it home for a little while.

Michaela wasn't there when I arrived. Which wasn't particularly unusual—we were our own women who did our own thing—but in that moment, it *was* vexing. I grabbed my kindle—all thanks be to Lilli and her magical touch with everything technological—and settled down on the sofa to wait.

I loved reading. Sometimes, the world grew too loud, too dark, too sad, and it was nice to shut it all out for a while. Even though I was a killer, and made no apologies for that, I really did try to stick as close as I could to my principles. Reading was a way to silence all the noise, like placing your thumb over the sun to blot out its screaming light. I'd been an avid reader for as long as I could remember, reading every genre without exception. Since sapphic books had become more widespread, I'd taken to devouring them almost exclusively. There was something freeing about being able to slip into a new world at the flick of a wrist. It was nice to experience the characters and their problems, because their problems were always solved by the turn of the last page.

I'd seen a lot of suffering in my long life—had been the cause of it too, I wasn't going to sugarcoat anything—and nothing beat slipping away for a few hours. Reading brought a peace unlike anything else. In all my five centuries, nothing had ever come close.

I was able to get lost in my book for an hour. Which, given that I'd devoted entire weeks to reading before, wasn't long. Not even an engrossing sapphic murder mystery could keep my mind from wandering back to Saira.

I was an idiot. It wasn't the first time I'd been driven to distraction by a human—and let's be honest, probably wasn't the last—but it *was* the first time the human was a hunter, and I liked to think I had adequate enough intelligence to know pursuing anything was a bad idea.

Apparently not.

Perhaps everything would be fine. I'd keep my people away from hers, and vice versa, and we could have our little dalliance until it ran its course. There was no harm in that, surely. It could even be fun. Sneaking around, fucking a hunter right under their noses. The element of danger hanging over it all was oddly alluring.

Or, much more likely, it would all come crashing down on our heads and one or both of us would die.

I sighed and forced myself to read another chapter. Anything to get Saira out of my head. Was she struggling with the whole thing like I was, or had she given in to the draw between us and decided to ride it out? *Maybe I should do the same.* Thinking in circles never got anyone anywhere.

My stomach rumbled.

I threw my kindle on the sofa and pinched my brow. Hunger lit up each and every nerve, as sudden and ubiquitous as stars rioting in the sky once the sun set for the night. I missed studying astronomy, but that was neither here nor there. My stomach clenched around nothing, and I inhaled deeply through my nose and let out a measured exhale through my mouth. Something else to add to my growing list of inconveniences. At least I'd narrowed down my list of potential victims.

Before I could start to worry about that too, the front door opened and Michaela strode through, carrying shopping bags. A *lot* of shopping bags. Honestly, since I'd shown her how to move the money she'd made at the Beyer corporation into untraceable accounts, she seemed determined to burn through it all as quickly as possible.

"Hey," she said, dumping the numerous bags on the living room floor. "Don't worry, it's not all for me. I got you a new jumper and some new jeans." She pulled said jumper out of a bag with a flourish and tossed it at me. The black material was soft and warm, and I knew it would be perfect for cozy days in, reading by a fire while wind and rain lashed the windows with wild fury.

"Thank you," I said, folding the jumper in my lap. "You didn't have to get me anything."

Michaela shrugged. "I like shopping. For myself and for others. I always bought the best gifts for Secret Santa. It's a real talent." She flipped her braids over a shoulder in a show of false haughtiness, making us both laugh.

She rummaged through the bags, pulling out items to show me, then folded them neatly at her side. She had good taste. Maybe she would go into fashion one day, but that industry had become entirely too high profile, so maybe not. The last thing any vampire needed was *fame*. Perish the thought.

"How did it go with your friend?" Michaela put aside a particularly beautiful dress, and I made a mental note to ask her where she'd bought it from. "Colette, right? The one you've known since forever?" Michaela, a little like Saira earlier, remained in awe of my age. Every time she asked me about something from decades or centuries ago, she always did so in a tone wrapped in amazement. I tried not to let it go to my head, but I didn't always succeed. Longevity didn't automatically bestow wisdom, but it was still nice to know she thought me wise.

"About that," I said, leaning forward, my elbows on my knees. "We need to talk."

Michaela took one look at my face and stopped going through her shopping. "What's wrong?"

"You know, back at the retreat," I started slowly, unsure as to how she would respond. She was an intelligent woman, and she knew I'd slept with Saira; she would put two and two together. "I told you a couple of hunters had escaped."

"Yeah," she said, wariness dragging the word out.

"One of them was Saira Masood, and she's here. She confronted us at the Botanical Gardens."

Michaela stood and started pacing the small room, her steps jerky and irregular, like she couldn't decide to keep walking or stop and yell at me. "Saria. The one who shot me. The one you slept with. I thought you'd killed her. Do you have feelings for her or something? Is that why she's still alive? How did she find us? Do we need to leave?"

Oh, *now* she wanted to leave. I almost rolled my eyes but managed to keep my expression neutral. "She didn't find us. As far as I'm aware, we're okay." I held up a hand to stall any more rapid-fire questions. "Listen, please. A group of hunters, including Saria, were tracking the group Colette is with. I just happened to be in the wrong place at the wrong time, and now she knows I'm here, too. This is kind of good news for you, actually."

Michaela raised a sardonic eyebrow. "Good news? How is any of this good news?"

"You wanted to stay, didn't you? Well, now we are."

Michaela stopped pacing and gaped at me, her disbelieving expression bordering on comical. "Are you serious? We know hunters are here, they know we're here, yet *now* you want to stay. Why? It's not because you want to fuck Saira again, is it?"

"No," I said, perhaps a little too quickly if the way Michaela's brows pulled down was any indication, and I bulldozed on before she could stop me. "It's about helping Colette. Making sure she gets away safely. Saira has nothing—"

My empty stomach chose that moment to loudly announce how empty it was. The thunder on Michaela' face dissipated into something more humorous. She pursed her lips, and I huffed out a breath.

"I also... I need to feed before we can move. Those bastards from a couple of months ago haven't sustained me for as long as I'd hoped."

Michaela dropped next to me on the sofa, collapsing back against the cushions like all her energy had deserted her at once. "Are you sure we haven't been burned?"

I didn't know how to tell her about mine and Saira's strange, unspoken agreement, that neither of us would go after the other—in the killing sense, at least—and nor did I want to. It was ours, and ours alone. I doubted Michaela would understand. She hadn't been a vampire for very long, but she knew to stay away from hunters. Perhaps I could learn a thing or two.

"I'm sure," I said in my most reassuring voice. "She only talked to me as a means of scaring Colette and Gracie away so hunters could tail them and find where they're staying. Gracie is with Colette's group. She came to the Gardens as well."

Michaela deflated like a puffer fish, dropping her head on the back of the sofa. "Okay. I still don't like this. Tell me everything that happened. *Everything*, this time, please. Then we can find you someone to eat. Someone horrible if we can, I know," she added when I opened my mouth to say just that. "You have such a bizarre set of morals for a vampire."

I rolled my eyes and told her... the majority. I certainly didn't reveal I'd exchanged numbers with Saira, or that we planned to meet. I'd already texted her, so she had my number too. It was all so alluringly *dangerous*. Michaela didn't need to know any of that.

We talked well into the evening, and by the time moonlight dominated the night sky, Michaela was in better spirits. We both were. She was happy we were staying for a little longer, and I'd convinced her not to worry too much about hunters. We'd troubleshooted places to look for food and I'd narrowed my list down even further. Everything was going to be fine.

All's well that ends well.

If I told myself that often enough, I wondered if I'd begin to believe it.

5

I craned my neck to look up at the sign outside the building. *John Murphy Bar*. The bottom part of the *y* had been knocked off some time in the bar's no doubt illustrious history, and rust covered the whole sign to the point it *had* to be permanently stuck on the wall. Noise flooded out through the closed door, the black paint peeling away to reveal old wood beneath. My sensitive ears begged for release, and I hadn't even set foot inside yet. Humans were so noisy and inconsiderate of others. My nose wrinkled as an assortment of smells assaulted me; alcohol, body odour, an amalgamation of fragrances that threatened to give me a headache, and underneath it all, the glorious aroma of blood.

I parted my lips ever so slightly and eased my fangs from my gums. The relief was instantaneous; a painkiller finally kicking that persistent ache away. I ran my tongue over my teeth as my stomach growled. Soon. Someone's blood would pour down my throat all hot and heady and magnificent. I clenched my fists against the rush of need. *Soon.*

For now, Saira came first.

Forcing my fangs away—no easy feat, let me tell you—I reached into the little, sequined bag I carried for my old flip phone. Most people would probably laugh, but protecting my identity mattered more than having the latest tech. I didn't want to carry an easily tracked computer in my pocket.

Saira, 15:11

> John Murphy Bar, 8pm tonight.

That was it. No other message, nothing about a dress code or what we were meeting for—although I had my hopes—and she hadn't replied to my response. A traitorous corner of my mind flashed a hazardous red, and I gave into its incessant warning. A quick loop around the bar showed nothing untoward. The building sat on a relatively quiet street, propped up by a pharmacy on one side and a barbers on the other. I didn't spot anything suspicious, and the red alarm flashing in my mind dimmed to a dull orange.

Back outside the peeling door, I ran a hand down my silver dress, fluffed up my blonde hair—I really needed to dye it soon, I'd kept it my natural colour too long—and stepped into the fray.

All my senses were immediately overloaded. Hearing and smell worst of all, but also sight; men made up the majority of the patrons, and I didn't particularly like looking at them, taste; alcohol lay heavy on the air, coating my tongue before I'd taken more than a few steps into the room, and touch; people invaded my personal space like they had a right to be there, and I did *not* like it. While I did go to bars, my time spent in them was infrequent. Gay bars sometimes for a quick hook-up, and straight bars sometimes for a quick feed. They were rife with pathetic men attempting to drug and assault women, and I took great pleasure in removing them from the world.

This bar seemed far busier than they usually were on a Sunday night. Had there been a football match on, perhaps? The only sport I followed with any regularity was the Olympics—the summer, winter, and Paralympic games—because I loved how ancient they were and because nothing beat watching a gymnast's control and precision. I'd tried gymnastics briefly. Turned out I was better at watching it than doing it, but the less said about that, the better.

I forced my way through the crowd towards the bar where dim purple lighting illuminated staff run ragged beneath shelves of alcohol. My head swivelled every which way as I searched for Saira. My little reconnaissance mission had made me a few minutes late, but it never crossed my mind that she'd leave. I would wait for her, and she would wait for me.

Where is she, where is—there.

I course corrected to the corner of the bar and paused for a moment to drink her in. She leaned against the shiny surface, wearing a nice, short sleeved T-shirt tucked into tight black jeans. I marvelled at the shape of her thighs, the curves of her body, dragging my eyes over the denim and wishing we were somewhere else so I could strip it from her skin. My stomach tightened with a different kind of hunger.

My eyes roamed over her arms—she *had* been working out, they were more toned than I remembered—and across to where her breasts were pushing up against her top, only to pause when a tingle passed over my skin. I raised my gaze and found her watching me, an eyebrow quirked in amusement. She'd caught me checking her out. Well, why not? She knew I was attracted to her. I refused to feel embarrassed by that.

Closing the gap between us, I leaned into her, our body heat entwining. My short dress was a bit much for the location, but I congratulated myself on my choice when Saira inhaled sharply, her eyes dropping to my cleavage. It was my turn to quirk an amused eyebrow, and I revelled in the rush of satisfaction her blush gave me.

"What are you drinking?" I asked, nodding to her empty hands.

She bit her lip and I had to calm myself down. Kissing her now was incompatible with the slow seduction I had planned. And if I was being completely honest with myself, and as depressing as the realisation was, the need for blood had too great a hold on me to take her to bed. I didn't want to hurt her.

"A Guinness, please."

"A Guinness?" I parroted, unable to contain my smirk. "Do you actually like it or is this a tourist thing? I've heard it's a very polarising drink."

She shrugged. "A tourist thing. Gotta try real Guinness when in Ireland. My dad is expecting a detailed review." Her smile was fond, and I put aside that information to ask about later. She was close to her parents. She'd told me they were ill back at the retreat, but that had probably been a lie.

I didn't hold it against her. Our lies back then had been necessary to safeguard our secrets. Now, though, something about her demanded truth. The thought of lying sat heavy on my chest, like the need for a deep breath but your lungs just wouldn't expand properly. You weren't suffocating, but it certainly felt like it. I'd do my best to be honest with her unless it hurt my kind, and I knew she'd do the same for me.

It didn't take long to get our drinks. A Guinness for Saira and a water for me. Some drunk idiots nearly knocked the glasses from my hands, but my reflexes were as brilliant as ever and I made it back to Saira with our drinks full and my dress unstained. Not for the first time, curiosity curled through me at the thought of being drunk. Back when I was human, I mainly drank water—the idea medieval peasants drank ale because all water was dirty and contaminated was a silly myth; yes, we didn't have germ theory, but we weren't stupid, thank you very much—and once wine, and believe it or not, I'd never actually been drunk in my entire five hundred and forty-one years of existence. Not that I could get inebriated now, of course. I'd vomit it back up before I could drink enough.

Saira knocked her glass with mine, and we took a drink together. My water tasted like nothing, but it helped wash away some of the sticky alcohol coating my mouth, and I could breathe a little easier. I looked back at Saira in time to catch her face contort into an impressive grimace, and she put her drink down with a little too much force.

I chuckled. "Not to your liking?"

"Ugh, no." She glared at the pint like she wanted to smash it into the bar. "People actually like that?"

"What did it taste like?" I asked, moving closer, partly to hear her better over the pervasive noise—I genuinely wanted to know—and partly because I wanted to feel more of her heat.

"Like roasted bitterness." Saira stole my water and downed half the glass. I cocked my head in amusement, and she angled hers right back, unrepentant.

I reached out and grabbed her Guinness, the drink still settling in the glass, black liquid vying against the creamy top. "Roasted bitterness. How interesting." It smelled awful. The strong scent blotted out everything else, and against my better judgment, I took a small sip.

Instant regret. Curiosity really did kill the cat.

My lips pulled into a snarl, and I had to fight my fangs, which pushed against my gums in protest of the foul drink. Why had I done that? What a fool. The bitterness smeared against my mouth like paint, sticky and viscous and sour, refusing my attempt to swallow it away. I downed the rest of my water in three quick gulps.

Saira laughed at me. "What did you do that for? What did it taste like?"

"Like death," I lamented, revisiting all my poor life choices. "I don't know why I did that."

"What does non-blood stuff taste like for you?" Saira asked, her body turned towards me, her expression open and interested. The purple light danced in the brown of her eyes, drawing me in like hypnosis.

"It varies." I mirrored her body language. "Sometimes it just tastes slightly off, sometimes it tastes rotten, sometimes it makes me violently sick. That tasted rotten."

Saira's lips pursed, ensnaring my gaze. I'd felt them before, tasted them, nibbled them, licked them, but it was so long ago, and I needed to do it all again. "The thought of drinking someone's blood makes me feel sick," Saira said as I dragged my mind away from sex, "so I guess it makes a perverse kind of sense that the opposite would be true for vampires."

"I'll get you another drink," I said, not wanting to linger on our differences.

"It's okay."

I shook my head. "No, let me get you something you'll actually enjoy. Can't have my woman unsatisfied." I shot her a wink, hoping she'd be more turned on than irritated by the '*my woman*' comment. I'd never been a possessive lover, but right then, and hopefully in the foreseeable future, Saira would be all mine.

She tapped a finger against her lower lip and looked to be fighting a smile. "Red wine, please."

It didn't take me long to return with more drinks, water for me, wine for her. The same type she'd brought to my room at the retreat.

She raised her eyebrows at the taste, and I knew she was thinking about our time there.

"I'm impressed you remembered this," she said.

"I'm a woman of many talents," I murmured, taking a sip of water.

"True." She hummed, a soft smile lighting up her face. "Did you know me coming to your room that night was a brief moment of insanity before I remembered my mission?"

"I thought you left because talking about travelling made you morose."

"That, too," she sighed. "But mainly the mission. I should have been tracking Michaela's movements, not trying to get into your bed."

I smirked at her. "Well, I'm glad you were trying to get into my bed. And I'm *very* glad I ended up in yours."

She had a sip of her wine but didn't return my smirk. Instead, her face turned... sheepish? It was the only word that came to mind. "What's wrong?"

"I have a question, and I hope I don't come across as jealous or clingy or something." She ended her sentence abruptly, taking another drink of wine. I had no clue what she wanted to ask, and intrigue tingled along my skin.

"Ask away. I promise I won't think of you as any of those things."

"When you were meeting the botanists yesterday, your friends," she started, stumbling over her words a little, "you seemed very close with the one in the maroon hoodie. Colette. You hugged for a long time. Which is fine, obviously but... God, it sounds even more ridiculous saying it out loud. We haven't even seen each other in over a year, and you don't owe me anything."

I squeezed her arm. I wasn't the first time potential lovers had picked up on me and Colette, and I'd never lied to anyone about us. How Saira reacted was up to her.

"Colette is..." I trailed off, unsure where to start. "We've known each other for centuries. It's difficult to quantify what we mean to each other after all this time. We've been friends since the day we met. We've been on and off lovers over the years. We've always been there for each other, no matter what. I'd drop what I was doing in a heartbeat if she asked me to, and the same goes for her if I asked. She's been a large part of my life for most of my life, and she's always going to be part of me. If that scares you, I need you to tell me now. But please know, yes, we love each other and that won't change, but in terms of sex and relationships, she's been in love with other people before, as have I, and we aren't jealous of that. Whenever we have relationships with people, we respect that. You don't have to feel threatened by her in any way. Right now, all I see is you. All I want is you. Like you said, it's been over a year since I last saw you, and you've been on my mind that entire time. *You*, not Colette."

I stopped before I could ramble on. It was hard for me to fit what Colette and I were in a neat little box for someone who didn't have the same perspective longevity gave us, and I wasn't sure I succeeded. Saira's middle finger kept tapping on her wine glass, but other than that, she gave no outward indication of her thoughts.

She stayed silent for a full minute, and I did my best not to fidget. I was a dignified and respectable lady, not some pathetic loser whose stomach twisted itself into knots waiting for her crush to say something. Say anything. Why wasn't she saying anything?

"I think I understand," she eventually said, the words walking past her lips slowly, like she was still going over everything in her mind. "You and her are..." she paused, but I understood. Colette and I defied labels. "You love each other, in every sense of the word, but you've also been around long enough to know that you're each your own woman, who will go off and do their own thing, including other people. You don't stifle each other. Which, I guess, if you're alive for centuries, will happen if you're around the same people all the time. Is that it?"

I nodded. It was a good enough explanation, I supposed. Colette and I had never *stifled* each other, but I didn't really know how to explain us further.

Saira leaned in, her breath tickling my neck. "As long as she understands that for now, you're all mine."

A shiver worked its way down my back. I *liked* possessive Saira. "Good," I said, a touch breathless. "And honestly, you really do have nothing to worry about from her. We—"

A loud cheer went up throughout the pub and dissolved into what I thought was a football chant. The crowd grew more rowdy with every passing second. Maybe Saira would want to leave with me? But no. My stomach was a gaping, ravenous void, the hunger growing harder and harder to ignore. Blood first, sex another night.

A real shame.

"Do you like sports?"

Saira whispered the innocuous question directly into my ear, apparently moving on from Colette. I'd expected more questions, but maybe she'd already accepted it. Or maybe she needed to think on it in her own time. Whatever it was, the way her lips brushed against the shell of my ear sent a spike of heat between my legs and blew all worries about Saira and Colette from my mind. For the first time in a long time, I cursed my need for blood. All I wanted to do was Saira, not hunt for some bastard to feed on.

I twisted back to face her. We were close enough that I saw her pupils dilate, black absorbing brown. I clamped down on the rush of want. I couldn't. Not tonight. It was so *frustrating*.

"I tried to get into American sports while I was over there," I said, keeping my voice light and as free of desire as I could make it, but I wasn't sure how successful I was. She was *so close*. Her lips were *right there*. "Things like baseball and basketball and American football. I found them boring, to be honest. The only sporting event I follow with any regularity is the Olympics. It's... nice, watching things older than me. Seeing them persisting, even flourishing." I stopped then, not wanting to remind her of my age. We weren't vampire and hunter in that bar, just two women getting to know one another better. "What about you?"

Saira's face scrunched up. *Adorable*. "No, I'm not a sports fan. Nothing ever really interested me. I ran track at school but that was it. Although now that you mention it, I'll watch the Olympics if other people are. My mom loves the swimming." Her smile was just as fond for her mum as it had been for her dad.

I told her about my love of the gymnastics, although I had no idea what I said, too distracted by the goosebumps all over my body and the almost unbearable tightness below my stomach. And Saira herself, of course. The way her mouth moved as she smiled in response to something I said; the way she glided her fingers over my arm yet didn't seem aware she was doing it, while there I was, getting more and more worked up; the way enjoyment danced in her eyes as she talked about one summer her parents and a bunch of friends all watched the swimming together, and her mum got so excited during the final that she threw her food and drink everywhere.

"Are you close to your parents?"

Saira nodded, her smile turning pensive. "Yeah, very, which always surprises people because I'm hardly ever home. I miss them."

"I'm sure they miss you too."

"Every time I go home my mom always makes my favourite food. Nihari, have you—" she cut herself off with a low chuckle. "I was going to ask if you've had it before, but obviously not. The soft beef, the blended spices, damn, you're missing out." She moaned at whatever memory she was lost in, and I *really* felt like I was missing out. I'd never given human food much thought before, but in that moment, I could honestly say I was jealous of nihari.

I pressed my thighs together and ignored the incessant pulse there. Tonight was about getting to know Saira better. "Is your mum a chef?"

"No," Saira said, shaking her head. "She's just really good at cooking. She works in HR for a company. She doesn't really like it, but it helps with the bills, as she always says." Again, her smile was fond. My own mother was nothing more than a familiar smell and soft singing voice, but I like to think I wore the same expression whenever I spoke of her.

"When I was young," Saira continued, "and my passion for geography and traveling became obvious, my mom started cooking food from other cultures too. Those glimpses meant everything to me. I loved coming home to a different part of the world after school." Her eyes clouded with nostalgia, and I could only stare at her. The purple light kept shifting into shadow as the crowd ebbed and flowed around us, lending her beauty an almost mystical quality, and I felt honoured that such a remarkable woman had deigned to share parts of herself with me.

I was so lost in her voice, in listening to small snippets of her life, that she took me by surprise when she downed her wine and stood from her stool. I blinked up at her, my mouth forming an 'o'.

"Fuck it," she whispered, "you can't look at me like that and not expect me to do anything about it." She cradled my chin and pulled me up to her.

I went eagerly, despite my earlier reservations. She pushed her body against mine like she'd been holding herself back from throwing me against the bar and having her way with me. The thought made my toes curl. Her hands gripped my waist, pulling our bodies flush together, and I slid my hands up her arms and around her neck, relishing the feel of her smooth, warm skin.

She nipped my lower lip then sucked it into her mouth. I couldn't have stopped the shiver that ran through me if my life depended on it. She released my lip after nibbling it between her teeth, and I wasted no time joining our mouths again. I ran my own tongue over her bottom lip, and she readily let me in. Her moan vibrated through my bones as I ran my tongue along hers, and I began to grow dizzy with arousal. The feel of her heat under my hands, the taste of her under my mouth, the smell of her body and blood all wrapped me in a tight bubble until all I could think was *Saira Saira Saira*.

A wolf-whistle burst that bubble. I dragged myself away from Saira to glare at the person who'd interrupted us. A group of four men wore matching lewd grins, and I instantly felt unclean. It was easy to forget, in Saira's presence, or the presence of any lesbian for that matter, that the majority of the world either hated us or fetishised us. My body grew rigid, and not even Saira's reassuring touch relaxed me. I wanted to rip the men limb from limb, gorging myself on their blood as they died begging for mercy—

"Come on." Saira tugged me away. "Let's get out of here."

I did my best to disregard their shitty comments and focus instead on the feel of Saira's hand in mine, but anger raged in my gut. My fangs dropped down, eager to tear through skin to get to hot, sweet blood. How dare those bastards taint what I had with Saira for their own gross amusement? I wanted to go back and destroy them so thoroughly, nothing but crumpled body parts remained. Sending a glare over my shoulder, I caught a glimpse of them laughing before they were engulfed by the crowd as Saira dragged me further away.

I took a deep, steadying breath in through my nose and let it out through my mouth, along with my fury. My stomach growled in protest as I tried to put them out of my mind, tried to think instead of Saira, of making her writhe and scream and gasp out my name. That was better.

"Why did you pick this bar?" I asked her as we made slow progress through the crowd. Maybe it was something as simple as she didn't know the area, but the pervasive hetero-ness was an annoyance I could have done without.

She shrugged, stopping as a group cut across in front of her. "I asked some of the guys at work for bar recommendations. This one was mentioned as a dive no one went to, so I thought it would be okay. Less chance of getting spotted." She threw a flirty smile over her shoulder. "To be honest, I only expected to stay for one drink, if that. There's a hotel not far from here."

My answering smirk was a little forced as she continued pulling me through the press. I needed blood, not sex, and those disgusting men had ruined the mood for me, besides. Hopefully Saira wouldn't be too disappointed.

6

We didn't make it out of the bar.

I was glaring around the pub, wishing Saira had done more research of Dublin and taken me to a gay bar instead of a straight hellhole, and wondering how to ask for a rain check on the hooking up, when I spotted it. Stopping suddenly, and dragging Saira to a halt with me, I narrowed my eyes at the couple.

A man with glasses and a redheaded woman were at a table near the door. Nothing unusual there, the place was crawling with straight people. The man had brought the woman a fresh drink. Beer for him, some kind of spirit for her. Again, nothing unusual. But as she got up to go to what I assumed was the restroom, the man pulled something out of his pocket and dropped it in her drink.

Contrary to what you might think, a peace settled over me. Tension unwound itself and my body relaxed even as my hunger sharpened. Him. I'd kill and drain him. Anticipation replaced annoyance, and even my eagerness for Saira faded at the thought of blood.

I was *really* hungry.

"Anna? What's wrong?"

I pointed the man out to Saira. "He's just put something in a woman's drink."

Her hand tightened in mine. "He did? Are you sure?"

"*Yes*, I'm sure. Come on."

I didn't give her a chance to respond before pulling her along with me. I was a vampire. I killed people to live, including women. But I also hated seeing violence against women, the majority of which was done by men. That made me a hypocrite, sure, but if I could save a woman, I would. Especially if it enabled me to rid the world of one more shitty man.

Elegance walked in step with me as I stalked forward. How you moved through the world was a big part of how the world responded to you, and *I* controlled my world, *not* the other way around. But just at the right moment, all my elegance and grace abandoned me as I stumbled and crashed into the table like a proverbial bull in a China shop, knocking the woman's drink all over the man.

I took great pleasure in his shocked shout. There were few things better than enraging an entitled arsehole before verbally and physically eviscerating them.

"What the fuck!"

"Oh no, I am *so* sorry," I said, laying it on thick. Saira stifled a laugh next to me.

"Watch where you're going next time. Fucking hell," the man grumbled, his anger diminished as he finally looked up at me. One good thing about my vampire enhanced beauty was that plenty of women noticed me. The cons were that men noticed me too. *Ugh*.

"I've two left feet, I'm afraid," I continued, all but throwing a napkin at him. "Here, why don't you pop to the toilets and get cleaned up, and I'll buy you another drink, how does that sound?"

He'd started nodding before I finished speaking. "Yeah, good. Another San Miguel." The way his eyes dragged over my body made me want to claw them out. "I'll be right back."

I tracked him all the way to the back corridor that led to the toilets. Good. I had a quick, internal debate with myself on whether to attack him there or lure him outside, but Saira's voice broke through my thoughts before a plan could fully form.

"Anna. You better not be doing what I think you're doing."

Her anger was a physical thing, muddying the air and pushing us apart. Gone was Saira the woman, who wanted to get as close as possible to me, and in her place was Saira the hunter, homing in on her vampire. "Come on." I pulled her after the man into the empty corridor.

"What are we doing here?" Saira asked, her low voice easier to hear in the relative quiet.

I didn't see the point of beating around the bush. She knew what I was. "I'm going to kill him."

She pinched her brow between her fingers. "That's what I thought you were going to say."

"Men who prey on women deserve to have their throats ripped out," I said, matter of fact.

Saira ground her jaw so hard I worried for her teeth. "So, what? You're just going to kill him now? Here?"

I hummed. "When you put it like that it doesn't seem like the best place, does it?" Where could I feed? The toilets? No. Not only was that gross, but the risk of someone walking in was too great. One of the back rooms, maybe? A storage room would do nicely.

"Look, I get it, okay?" Saira said through clenched teeth, her face pinched. I took that to mean she was conflicted, which meant I could sway her to my way of seeing things. "The oath I took when I joined the hunters does sometimes war with my reality as a woman. A brown woman at that, so I *get it* way more than you *ever* will. I'm a good fighter, I can hold my own, but I still cross the road if a group of men are coming toward me. Or sometimes I walk with earphones in without playing music, just so I can hear if I'm being followed. If I'm ever out at night, I tend to stick to the crowds as often possible, so I won't be caught somewhere alone. And guess what? I've been harassed in broad daylight too, because of the colour of my skin, because of my gender, because some random man feels insecure or threatened or whatever, so they take it out on women. Especially women like me. So don't *ever* patronise me again about violence against women."

My heart went out to her. Women's safety had improved since I was young, but it still left a lot to be desired, especially for women of colour.

I reached out and laced my fingers with hers. "I'm *sorry*. I never meant to be condescending in any way. It's more awful than I can truly express. That heightened sense of awareness just to walk down a street. That extra burst of speed to get home more quickly. The way fear drips between your shoulder blades when you hear someone behind you." I shook my head, the fury inside me increasing to a white-hot inferno. "You agree," I continued, "I'll kill him, and there's one less sexual predator in the world."

"I *understand*," Saira emphasised. "He should be locked up, the key conveniently lost, but not murdered."

I tilted my head to the side. "You have the death penalty in America. I'm just cutting out the middleman."

"The death penalty is for murderers. Besides, he technically hasn't done anything. You stopped him in time."

"Murder can be accidental, or in self-defence. But rape? That is one hundred percent intentional. It's a revolting thing to do to someone, and he *is* going to die for it. How do we know he hasn't done it before? Or that he will in the future? Him spiking that drink looked practiced to me."

She pulled her hand from mine and glared at me. "For the record, I really hate that you're putting me in the position of playing devil's advocate for such a shitty person. I agree with what you've just said. I think what he did is disgusting. But my oath won't let me let *you* straight up murder him."

There it was. She *did* agree with me. She was just hung up on some oath I hadn't even known hunters took.

"I take it the gist of this oath is to protect humans from vampires?" I asked, unable to keep my eye roll under wraps. "Hunters do know the world isn't all black and white, yes? That humans can be just as monstrous, often more so, than us, right?" I sighed, reaching for her hand again. She let me take it, the challenge fading somewhat from her eyes. "I don't mean to make this difficult for you. It's just... I need blood to live. You eat meat, I'm assuming? Do you give a second thought to the animal it came from?"

Confusion clouded her gaze. "You're comparing humans to animals?"

"No." I ran my tongue over my teeth. "I'm just saying, animals can think, experience emotions. Just because they don't have '*higher thoughts*' doesn't make them less deserving of life. Yet you still eat them. Humans rear them for the sole purpose of killing them for food. What I'm saying, badly, I'll grant you, is that I need human blood to survive. Just like you eat meat to survive. Why not the blood of an awful man who was going to attack someone over that of a truly innocent person?"

Saira blinked and looked away, the corners of her eyes crinkling as she scrunched her face up. "You make a... halfway decent point," she said, her voice so quiet even I had to lean closer. Her expression turned inward, like she was looking at the deepest parts of herself. "You know, there's a big part of me that's always loved the hunt, the kill. I used to wonder why I didn't recoil from it more, but I grew to accept it. That part of me is saying: yeah, let her kill him. One less predator is a good thing. The other part of me, the one that swore the oath, is telling me to try and stop you." She met my eyes and I saw none of the conflict her words suggested. "But it doesn't matter, does it? I made my decision when I gave you Justin Stewart back at the retreat." She shook her head, laughing a little to herself. I could only watch, mesmerised. "I was stretched over the coals for that, y'know, but I managed to spin it as more of a *'him or us'* situation than it had been. As soon as you said he was an abuser I knew it was truth. I'd heard rumours that he used to beat his wife and kids during my time there, but nothing concrete. And I just... gave him to you. And you know what? I didn't lose a single second of sleep over it. Does that make me a monster too?"

"No," I whispered, unable to utter anything louder. I remembered that delicious darkness I'd glimpsed in her at the Beyer retreat, and couldn't hold myself back from stepping into her space. "It makes you perfect."

I leaned in to kiss her right as the restroom door opened and Spike Man stepped through. He blinked at us, and as his repulsive lips started to curl into a smirk, I wiped it from his face with a punch to the stomach. He doubled over, winded, and I took the opportunity to bang his head against the wall. Not too hard, mind. I didn't want to kill him right away.

He slid down the wall, blinking in confusion and struggling to catch his breath. Not giving him a moment to even think about recovering, I grabbed under his arms and heaved him up. He let out a pained whine that made me wish I'd hit him harder.

I turned to Saira, who watched the whole thing in silence, her face unreadable. "You don't have to see this next part."

Her unreadable face grew alarmed. "You're not going to do it here, are you?"

"No." I didn't elaborate. We'd been in the corridor too long already and I didn't want to push my luck more; someone was bound to walk in any second. I hiked Spike Man further up off the floor and began dragging him down the hallway. "Are any of these back rooms empty?"

For a moment, Saira did nothing but stare after me, her jaw clenching and unclenching. She drew in a deep breath, and I heard her sigh even from down the corridor and over the noise of the bar. She strode past me and Spike Man, not sparing us a look as she started checking doors.

There were only four. One lead to the kitchens, which she quickly shut again. One was locked. One led to a walk-in cupboard that was so rammed full of boxes I couldn't fit in on my own, never mind with Spike Man. The last one led outside.

The wide alley was empty of people and full of bins and rubbish. The chill in the night slapped my cheeks, rudely reminding me that I *hated* the cold. Gritting my teeth against the biting air, I dragged Spike Man out and let him flop to the ground, where he started letting out little distressed noises as he pushed himself to his knees. I ignored him, turning back to Saira instead.

She spoke first. "This is not how I thought this night would go."

I breathed out a laugh. "I, unfortunately, imagined something not too dissimilar, to be honest. I'm really hungry. I didn't imagine you watching, though." The night had taken on more of a voyeuristic nature than I'd expected.

Saira tilted her head to the side, confusion shading her face. "So," she said, drawing the word out, "you didn't want to sleep together again?"

"Of course I do," I rushed to clarify. Maybe a little too quickly, but my ego didn't care. "I've just been ignoring my hunger while I tried to find people worth killing, and it's snuck up on me."

Saira's lips parted as something like revelation settled over her. "People worth killing?" she echoed. "What, you only kill 'bad' people?" She didn't move, but I heard the air quotation marks all the same. "Like the oil executives and this predator. Is that your MO?"

I shrugged. "Even monsters can have morals. I try to stick to mine as much as I can. It's not always possible, of course, situations can change rapidly, but I try my best." I didn't lose sleep over all the innocent people I'd fed on throughout the centuries, but I honestly did go for the dregs of society whenever possible.

"The world isn't black and white," Saira muttered. She gestured behind me to Spike Man, who'd been attempting to crawl away as we talked. I frowned at him. He should have been up and running at this point. Maybe I *had* hit him too hard. With a mental shrug, I hauled him up by his shirt. He let out another pained whine, his breathing short and laboured. I'd *definitely* hit him too hard. Why were humans so fragile?

"You don't have to watch this part."

Saira didn't look away. Not when I pulled Spike Man's head to the side and exposed his carotid artery. Not when I released my fangs. Not when I tore into his throat, hot blood spraying out. Not when my eyes slid shut as my stomach began to fill and Spike Man's struggles faded. Her eyes were still locked on me when I finished draining him, his lifeless corpse falling at my feet. My hunger was still a bright, burning light, but it wasn't quite as blinding anymore.

Saira only looked away when a noise alerted us both to another presence in the alley. She spun on her heel, her hands going up in a placating gesture as a woman stepped out of the shadows next to the door, tranquiliser gun clutched firmly in a fist.

"What the fuck's going on here, Boss?"

7

I cursed myself for not hearing her. Some vampire I was. I'd been so caught up in feeding that I'd ignored what my other senses had been trying to tell me. The smell of her blood and sweat flooded my nose, the faint tick of her heart tickled my ears. In my admittedly flimsy defence, the sounds of the pub were loud and distracting and drowned a lot of the woman out.

"Sam," Saira said, her hands still up. "Put the gun down."

The woman—Sam—didn't move. Her pale skin and black hair gave her a sallow look, and the bruises under her eyes only highlighted her ill appearance. For a relatively young human, she looked as weathered as a cliff face. I briefly wondered what she'd been through in her short existence, but my attention was bolted to the tranquiliser gun, and my pity for her was only slightly above non-existent.

She had to be one of Saira's team. Why had she followed her? How much had she seen? How much trouble was Saira in? Sam didn't look well—maybe I could use that to my advantage. That gun posed a very real threat, however, and I held myself as still as a statue. The unsteady shadow in Sam's eyes said I'd have a dart in me if I so much as twitched.

"Help me understand, Boss," Sam said, her voice cracking with uncertainty. She still referred to Saira as boss, which could only be a good thing. Saira still had authority. How would she spin everything? I held my tongue. The last thing I wanted was for the night to become even worse. Saira knew Sam; best let her control the narrative.

"Did you follow me here?" Steel was softer than Saira's tone.

Sam nodded. "When you said you were going out, I don't know, something seemed off. You didn't take your weapon. I wanted to make sure you were okay."

"I haven't taken my weapon with me the majority of the time I've gone out here, Sam. Guns are banned here."

"I know that." Sam shook her head, brandishing her weapon at me. "But you're meeting a vamp. You said she was an informant? I looked her up. She's not in any database."

Self-righteousness briefly blotted out my other emotions. I was *excellent* at avoiding detection. The hunters, despite numerous brushes with them, the closest being last year, still didn't have a record of me. I couldn't wait to tell Colette and Michaela. Maybe it would make Michaela listen to me when it came to moving around. I almost snorted. Somehow, I doubted that.

Saira stilled, her body holding a tension that seemed unnatural. "Why were you looking up my informants? Why are you questioning my information at all?"

"I question everything, you know that." Sam's eyes never left me, but she also couldn't meet my gaze. Like she wanted to keep watch but didn't want to acknowledge that I was a real person she could talk to. I'd seen it before. Hunters loved to dehumanise us, for lack of a better phrase. Make us nothing more than the monsters in their stories. I was more than willing to be the villain in Sam's, but I didn't want to darken Saira's doorstep with more trouble. And by the look of things, she was already in more than enough shit without me pushing her in deeper.

"You do," Saira said, her voice softer. Was she trying a different approach? "You always were a stickler for the rules, and it's helped us more times than I can count. You found and followed the botanists to the Gardens. It wasn't your fault they got away."

I'd known Colette had escaped in the core of my being—I honestly believed that after so long together I'd feel if she died—but hearing confirmation made my knees weak. I must have moved slightly, as Sam shuffled half a step forward.

"Don't," she growled. Her gun never wavered.

Saira half-turned, her gaze locking on mine, the set of her eyes telling me to go along with whatever she was about to say. I didn't respond, but I hoped she understood that *I* understood.

"Look," Sam said, her sunken eyes briefly flicking over to Saira before landing back on my left shoulder. "I wasn't sure if I should've followed you or not and only got here about a half hour ago. When I saw you two were... cozy, I was going to leave." A faint downward pull of her mouth told me she either didn't approve of gay people—which, tough shit. We've existed since forever—or she simply didn't approve of me. I didn't care which it was. I *did* care about that bloody gun still trained on my chest.

"Except... I don't know," Sam continued, her mouth turning even more down. "Something didn't feel right. It's not professional to have relationships with our informants, and in the year I've known you, you've been nothing *but* professional." Sam's shoulders gave a curious jolt that I belatedly realised was a shrug. The jerky movement caused the gun to shift ever so slightly. I kept my smile to myself. Lactic acid would make her muscles start to weaken, and I held patience close to my chest. The moment she faulted—the *moment*—would be her last.

"So, I followed you out here." A puzzled shadow passed over Sam's waxy face. "I accidentally knocked into someone in my rush to keep you both in sight, and it took a little while to get the guy off my back, but I finally got outside and saw..." she trailed off, her expression warring between confusion and resolve. Like she wanted to believe the best in Saira but couldn't deny what she'd witnessed.

I once again cursed myself for not hearing Sam, and wondered how Saira was going to play this. What kind of consequences would this have for her? *Should I kill Sam? I should kill Sam.* I settled into my patience, content to wait the humans out. Killing the hunter would be beneficial for both of us.

"Did you know?" Sam asked, a faint tremor in her voice. "That she's a vampire?"

My vampirism allowed me to pick up even the faintest of heart beats, but the silence following that question was so absolute I was sure the humans could hear each rapid beat as well.

Saira's shoulders jolted as she sucked in a jagged breath. "What I'm about to say goes way above your clearance level, do you understand?"

Sam's eyes once again flickered to Saira, her confusion even more evident. I shared it. I didn't know what tale Saira was about to spin. It was quite exciting.

"Yes."

Saira nodded a couple of times, like she wanted to emphasise how much she was deliberating over something. Saira's acting abilities back at the retreat had fooled everyone, and it was nice to see them in action again. I struggled to keep my face free of any creeping curiosity.

"The Irish Guild shared some information with me about a recently turned vamp who essentially hates what she's become," Saira said, her voice strong and brokering no argument. She waved a hand at me. "Anna here was turned against her will—" actually true, although she didn't know it, "—and has been helping them track down other vamps. Her details were passed to me as she knew some of our botanists." She shook her head, and I abruptly wished she wasn't facing away from me. I wanted to watch the deception play out across the plains of her face, shine bright in the depths of her eyes, etch itself into the contours of her lips. Sam's eyes were fully locked on Saira now, her frown expanding the sharp lines of her face. Did she buy Saira's lies?

"This is a massive secret that the Irish Guild has kept for years," Saira said, steel entering her voice again, "and I can't have you fucking it all up. They were reluctant to tell me at all, but you know how much I've nagged them for resources. Imagine if it got out? Hunters teaming up with vampires? It goes against the core of who we are and what we fight for." Saira shook her head, and I wondered what thoughts were running around in there. Did it go against the core of who she was to be with me? Somehow, given her actions, I didn't think so. Maybe there was more monster in her than I'd realised. If she became any more perfect, I was going to swoon.

"Only certain members even know about Anna," Saira continued, "never mind that she's a vampire. That's why she's not on any database. I know you love rules and structure, Sam, and that you think all information should be freely and equally shared, but *please*, keep this to yourself for now. Adrian and Julian can't find out. You know they couldn't keep a secret even if a million dollars were on the line."

A sardonic note had entered Saira's tone, like she was sharing an inside joke with Sam. An excellent way to draw her in. Make her feel included, privy to important information, and she would be less likely to betray Saira. Adrian and Julian were probably other members of their team, and by the sounds of it, they were shoot first and don't ask questions later types. Standard hunter grunts.

Sam lowered her gun. Instead of pointing at my chest, the muzzle hovered somewhere around my feet. My chest expanded a touch easier. Had Saira actually gotten through to her?

"I..."

No, she hadn't. Sam's pinched eyes darted between me and Saira, her confusion *more* prominent, not less. Saira had a better understanding of Sam and her temperament than me, but I decided to speak up anyway. Sam wasn't convinced, and I didn't think I could make it worse. I hoped, at least.

"This man," I gestured vaguely to where I'd dropped Spike Man, "was a sexual predator who had spiked a woman's drink. I need blood to live. I think this is a good outcome for everyone, don't you?"

"I did watch you spill a drink over him," Sam said slowly, like she was trying hard to believe us, but still couldn't quite get there.

I decided to keep pushing. "The people I killed before him were human traffickers. And before them, I fed from a couple of men who I'd overheard joking about beating their wives." That was a lie. I mean, I *had* killed a couple of men who were horrible domestic abusers, but that had been ten months ago. The people before the traffickers had been innocent of anything as far as I'd been aware, but I'd been hungry, and while we'd been walking through a park Michaela had lost control of her bloodlust and killed seven teenagers who had been drinking under some trees. I'd chewed her out over that; not only did the authorities start a massive manhunt for them—I'd given her an important lesson in hiding bodies and cleaning up a crime scene that night—but the missing kids had garnered national media attention.

I didn't like killing kids. I'd drilled that into Michaela that night. I remembered the bloodlust all too well though, even after centuries, and didn't fault her too much. She would have fed on anyone that night; the kids had simply been in the wrong place at the wrong time.

"A vamp with a conscience? Never heard of that before."

Sam's face was hard, her sunken eyes dark as coal. We were losing her. Not that we ever really had her. I should have kept my mouth shut.

"Sam—"

"No, Saira," Sam cut her off, and the use of Saira instead of Boss didn't go unnoticed. "If that's all true, fine. I find it hard to believe but I'll go along with it until we speak to the higher ups at the guild." She met my eyes for the first time since she burst out of the shadows and ruined my evening. "If it turns out you're both lying, Saira, you'll be charged with treason against your own species—" the words were spat, like it was the worst thing anyone could ever do, "—and you'll be locked away for the rest of your life. As for you," she turned back to me, using that bloody gun to point at my chest, like it was an extension of her hand, "we'll find you. No matter how far you run, how long you live, we'll find you." Her threat came off as a toddler scolding an adult, but that didn't stop the shiver running up my back. Real passion lit her up. I had no doubt she would do her best to be true to her word.

Sam turned to Saira again. "None of that explains why you're making out with her and letting her kill people in front of you. What's up with that?" Was that a note of hurt in her voice? I definitely heard disgust. Loathing. The kind of revulsion reserved for paedophiles and serial killers. I wondered what my kind had done to her.

Saira hesitated. She ran her hands over her jeans like they were sweaty, and I couldn't tell if she was genuinely stressed or still acting. "Look..." she sighed. "It's stupid."

Okay, she was still acting. I was more than impressed, and I only saw the back of her body. The fake tension in her shoulders, the phoney hesitation in her speech, the false reluctance to open up. I felt quite privileged to witness it. Maybe I'd ask her for acting lessons later.

"Just tell me," Sam said, each word bitten off.

"You know I'm a lesbian." Saira waited for Sam's nod before continuing. Her earlier disapproval was me then, not our gayness. "Well, I was like you when I first met Anna. Sceptical, cynical, didn't believe it at all. Why would a vamp help us hunt other vamps? She had to be playing some game. But I don't know, we spoke for a while about the botanists, and ended up talking about other stuff too, and I guess we hit it off. I mean, have you seen her?"

I smirked, satisfaction blossoming beneath my ribs. I knew I was attractive, but it never hurt to hear. Especially from Saira.

Sam's expression took on a doubtful colour. "You're just horny?"

Saira planted her hands on her hips, radiating discomfort. "See, it sounds stupid when you put it like that."

Sam lowered her weapon entirely, her body losing some of its stiffness, like Saira being hot for me had shocked all the suspicion out of her. Saira had woven a tale so implausible, so far-fetched—I mean, I'd never heard of any vampire in my entire life who'd willingly helped hunters—yet Sam actually seemed to be considering it. Why? What had Saira done to earn such loyalty? Or was Sam playing us now? Whatever it was, she stuffed her gun into the small of her back and rearranged her shapeless hoodie to conceal it.

I quickly made sure my face was an impassive mask. I wanted to gawk at them both but that would give the game away. A part of me had expected Sam to shoot, the residual adrenaline filling my muscles to the brim, and I had to force myself to stay as casual as possible when all I wanted to do was flop.

"C'mon," Saira said, gesturing Sam down the alley. "We'll walk back to HQ together. You have more questions, right?" She turned to me after Sam's weak nod. "You okay?" I gave a firmer nod and watched as Saira collected Sam. Together, they walked down the alley and out of my sight. Only then did I drop my aloof exterior.

I sagged against a wall like a discarded doll, still unable to believe everything that had happened. What a night. Something didn't sit right, and I didn't like the uncomfortable lump in my throat. Sam had conceded way too quickly. I wasn't in the habit of making friends with hunters, but I'd known enough of them to know the majority *despised* vampires. I didn't know Sam, but I didn't think she'd accept Saira was just horny for me. Hunters didn't have sex with vampires. We were abominations to them. Of course, there had been exceptions to the rule—see Saira—but in general, we hated them, they hated us.

I considered following them to find their headquarters, but I had a body to get rid of. Indecision held my limbs hostage. Dispose of the body, or tail Saira and Sam? Why not both?

The large rubbish bins wouldn't do. On the rooftop, maybe? The pub was only two stories, an easy jump for me, but no. Other buildings were taller, and someone would spot the body sooner or later.

Where? Precious seconds trickled away. The smell of their blood was already fading, diffusing into the maelstrom of scents that made up life.

A drain caught my eye. It was too small for him to fit through, but I was more than capable of ripping him apart and shoving him down it. Yes. The water and sewage would damage the body and hopefully he would be carried far from here.

Plan in place, I got to work.

8

They weren't difficult to find, but keeping myself hidden was another story. I still wore my revealing dress, and while I'd cleaned most of the blood off with Spike Man's shirt, a stain still sat on my left shoulder like one of those little devil cartoons, quite obviously blood. Not my best work, but hunger makes fools of us all. My high heels were the opposite of quiet and quickly became gorgeous annoyances on the ends of my feet. *And* I still carried my little bag with my old phone in. Not the best outfit for stealthily following people trained to kill me, but it wasn't like I had time to nip back home and change.

I couldn't get close enough to hear what they were saying. Considering it was after ten on a Sunday night, I couldn't really get close enough to keep them in sight, never mind eavesdrop. The streets were empty, the moon was bright, and my ears and nose took precedence over my eyes.

Nonetheless, they were fairly easy to follow. Their heartbeats were loud in the otherwise quiet night, and their blood drew me forward like metal to magnets.

Hunger still had its claws in me.

We walked for maybe half an hour. My heels had gone from gorgeous to grotesque. I stopped, ripped them off my feet, and threw them on the roof of some random building. Going barefoot was bliss compared to the agony of the last few minutes. I'd lived through the use of many torture devices, and in that moment, I ranked heels up there with the worst of them.

I pulled up short at a corner they'd rounded a minute ago. Numerous heartbeats drummed in my ears, like rain on a window, and I knew we'd arrived. Carefully sticking my head around the corner—I didn't know what kind of security a hunters building would have, and I wasn't about to announce myself to them—yet another empty street greeted me. The buildings looked more office than residential, and while I hadn't seen which one Saira and Sam had disappeared into, I knew it was one across the road made with faded yellow brick. The building itself was small and squat, no more than three stories high, with small windows and PRESTON & CO. stamped above the double doors in obnoxiously large letters. Some kind of front for the hunters, obviously. Everything about the place screamed *'don't bother committing us to memory, we're not worth the effort'*. I supposed most guilds across the world would be similar. People were less likely to remember slightly-below-average things, especially run down office buildings.

I'd never been to a hunter's guild headquarters, if you could believe that. Five centuries on this planet, and I'd done my best to avoid them as if they were all infested with the plague. Horrendous disease, by the way. The Black Death was before my time, but I did see numerous subsequent outbreaks, and the smell alone isn't something one easily forgets. Antibiotics were the closest humanity had ever come to a miracle.

I'd known several vampires over the years who'd stormed various guilds. Some successful, some not. I hadn't known any since the invention of those awful darts. Not that attacking the Dublin guild crossed my mind. I didn't have a death wish, thank you very much. No. Just maybe, possibly, somehow sneaking in and killing Sam. Or better yet, waiting until she left again so I didn't have to risk getting caught and killed. Even across the street and around a corner was too close for comfort.

I sighed, my breath rushing out like it couldn't wait to escape my lungs. In truth, I didn't know what to do. Sam knew my face, my name. She was probably adding me to their system at that very moment. For all I knew, Saira had been arrested and a bunch of hunters were gearing up to come after me.

I'd never been in a similar situation before, and while panic didn't have me quite in its clutches, it lurked at the back of my mind, its breath ghosting over my neck.

I should have done some sort of reconnaissance around the surrounding area, but every heartbeat came from the same yellow building, and I didn't want to get caught by some random hunter I'd somehow missed. I was skilled and experienced, but I'd seen coincidence take out far more of my kind than you'd think, and I didn't want that to happen to me. The embarrassment alone was enough to keep me stationary.

I leaned against cold brick and tilted my head to the sky. The few stars that pierced the light pollution winked at me. The night used to be a riot of stars and beauty that modern living had destroyed. Maybe after I dealt with everything in Dublin, I'd take a trip to the countryside, reconnect with nature and recuperate from what was probably going to be a harrowing ordeal.

I ran my tongue over my teeth. Seemed my subconscious had made up my mind for me. I wasn't leaving the city until I knew if I was on record, and if I was, all trace of me needed to be purged.

A shudder tore through me, partially because the night had to be below freezing—I was more resilient to temperature and weather than humans, but that didn't mean I wasn't affected, especially in a skimpy dress—and partially because I knew the next few days or weeks were going to be hard.

I'd ask Saira first. Hopefully she could erase all trace of me and that would be that. I didn't want to put her in unnecessary risk however, so if she said she couldn't, I'd take her word for it. If that was the case... I didn't know. Get together with Colette and throw some ideas about. She'd want to help me. She was *undeniably* in their records, and if we could do something about it, she would be first in line.

Mind made up, I turned to leave when the acceleration of a car and the underlying pulse of four heartbeats caught my attention. My shoulders jumped to my ears, and I had to force myself to relax and ease my head back around the corner.

A car pulled out of an underground garage entrance, and I caught a glimpse of the driver as they turned onto the road.

Sam. *Shit*.

She hadn't believed Saira. I hoped she could be convinced but something about her bruised eyes told me it wasn't possible. I didn't know what my kind had done to her, but whatever it was, Sam saw us as monsters to be eradicated and nothing else.

The decision to kill her was an easy one. She knew me, she knew Saira was involved with me, and letting her live would be a colossal mistake on par with Archduke Franz Ferdinand's driver making a wrong turn.

Well, not quite *that* bad, but you get the picture.

I followed the car as best I could. There was no doubt in my mind that the moment any of them saw me they'd shoot those infernal tranquiliser weapons, so while keeping pace was easy, I didn't get too close. A growl caught in my throat. Running bare foot on hard, cold asphalt was *not* pleasant. My mood soured with each step. I blamed Sam for the fact I was running after a car with no shoes on instead of being wrapped up in the searing warmth of Saira. Why did hunters always ruin everything?

Their destination was obvious. Back to the John Murphy bar. Had Sam brought a team, thinking I would still be there? Maybe she thought she could pick up my tail and find where I lived. Fat chance.

It wasn't often a group of hunters strolled into my lap, and I wasn't going to squander the opportunity to rid the world of four of them.

By the time I made it to the pub, the car blocked the entrance to the alley. I ducked around the corner and crouched next to the car, grabbing my first good look at the lot of them.

Sam stood off to the side with her arms crossed, looking like a pissed off drill sergeant as the other three hunters buzzed around in full body forensic suits. So, she was hoping to find Spike Man, maybe spot a trail I'd left. I scoffed. Did she think this was amateur hour? As if I'd leave a trail.

I waited, nestled between the brick of a building and the metal of the car, my bag tucked behind a wheel. Their heartbeats filled my ears, and as the smell of them curled up my nose, I eased my fangs from my gums. The relief was as palpable as my growing anticipation.

Three, two, one...

I burst out from my hiding place, taking vicious delight in the way the three forensic hunters scrambled in shock. One even fell over. Fool. I descended on him first, grabbing both arms and yanking him to my waiting fangs. He died before he could scream.

Blood streaming from my mouth, I kept my hold on Dead Forensic Man and charged at another hunter, this one scrambling around in fear whilst somehow staying in one spot.

Sam discharged her weapon four times. One dart went wide of everyone, and three lodged themselves into Dead Forensic Man. My lips curled into a wild grin. There were some benefits to men after all. I threw him at Sam—I don't think I'd ever grow tired of launching hunters around like they were bowling balls—and attacked Alive Forensic Man, who didn't stay alive for very long.

Neither did Alive Forensic Woman, who I killed while Sam clawed her way out from under the body I'd thrown.

I didn't give her a second to recover. Ignoring the blood from the three dead bodies, I reached around Sam and pulled the gun from her grip. Making sure she was watching, I crushed it and tossed it aside.

We stared at one another in silence for a beat or two as she pushed herself back to standing. I let her rise. She was no threat to me without her weapon, and I'd give her the dignity of dying on her feet.

"I knew it," she hissed, her jaw clamped so tightly shut it was a wonder any sound came out at all. "Every word Saira said was bullshit. Is she a vamp too? Did you turn her? When?"

I ignored the rapid-fire questions. I didn't owe her answers to mine and Saira's odd relationship. She, in turn, didn't owe me answers to all the questions I had, and the realisation that she wouldn't give me anything dawned as suddenly as a light being switched on. Best to feed and leave.

"Y'know, she almost had me convinced," Sam continued, still through gritted teeth. "That whole spiel about you hating what you'd become was pure lies, of course, I've never known a vamp work with hunters. But about her wanting you? That I knew was truth." She shook her head, disbelief etched all over her face. "I saw the way you interacted at the bar. You were all over each other. So, which is it? Is she a traitor to her species or did you turn her? When did you get to her? How much information about us has she told you?"

I tilted my head. "Saira is none of your concern."

"Fuck you."

I licked blood from my lips, debating whether or not to lean into Sam's assumptions. It *would* be funny to let a hunter think one of their own had been turned.

"She was a great hunter. Killed so many vamps," Sam snarled, and my patience ran out.

"And now, she'll kill a lot of hunters."

Sam's mouth twisted further. "You won't last. I've told others about you. I've added you to our system. Marked you as high priority. Dangerous, operating in Dublin, hunters and hunter's guild potentially compromised. You'll be killed, like the rest of your sick kind."

She continued ranting at me, but her words didn't reach my ears. I was on their system. They knew me. For the first time in my life, hunters *knew me*. I would *not* accept that. I already looked over my shoulder too often; a life where hunters knew my face was unimaginable.

I killed her quickly, tearing through her delicate skin and drinking down her delicious blood. She struggled, of course, I wouldn't expect anything less from a hunter, but in the end, it was another nice feed. My hunger receded a little more as I drank from the other three too.

With my hands on my hips, I contemplated the bodies. *Do I dump them somewhere or take them back to the guild as a sick joke?* Both options ran in circles through in my mind. Going back to the guild was too risky. Dumping them somewhere far away would be better.

It was well into the early hours of Monday morning before I finally made it home. After the quickest shower in history I collapsed on my bed and sleep swept me under almost instantaneously.

9

I sat at the kitchen table, staring at an imperfection in the wood. The kitchen normally saw little to no use—obviously, what would a couple of vampires use a microwave for? —but there I was, taking up space and doing nothing with it. The room was small and rectangular, the walls painted a rather garish yellow, and even I recognised the cupboards as old-fashioned. We used the living room much more frequently; I liked to sit in the over-stuffed armchair in the corner by the electric fireplace and read, the soft blue walls calming, especially on an evening, while Michaela settled on the sofa backed against the stairs and flicked through various news channels across different countries. She liked to keep informed, she said. She also had stock market information playing most days. I knew enough about it all to keep my money safe and secure—I'd hate to lose everything I'd accumulated over the centuries—but having it on all the time was a little excessive.

The space we'd carved out for ourselves was nice. I liked the little cushion on my seat, liked the abstract art hanging in the hallway that the landlord told us not to touch, liked my mornings spent chatting with Michaela. I'd enjoyed my time in Ireland, quite to my surprise. I'd grown used to hot weather, to larger spaces, more lavish houses, extravagant amenities. I enjoyed walk in wardrobes for all my clothes, not the tiny cupboard in my bedroom upstairs. I liked lots of shelves for my jewellery. I *really* liked—

My thoughts ground to a halt. I'd grown up poor, my family had next to nothing, and I'd always resented the aristocracy and upper classes. Had I... become them? Those rich bastards I'd always hated? I had more money than I knew what to do with, money begets money after all, despite donating to a lot of charities. Anonymously, of course. I wouldn't want hunters to find me because I'd left a paper trail of contributions to LGBTQ organisations, women's shelters, aid for people in war torn areas, you get the picture. Although, it would possibly make them see vampires as slightly less than devils incarnate. I mean, I *recycled*. That would blow their little minds. They wouldn't be able to handle such a challenge to their world view. Fanatics rarely did. And that's what hunters were. Fanatics. With the odd exception.

My thoughts were all over the place. Clearly my mind wanted to distract me from what I really needed to think about, which was hunters and guilds and somehow getting into one, erasing information, and getting out again, all without being captured and killed. And in order to do that, I needed—

"Salut, mon amour!"

Colette burst into the kitchen through the back door, all radiant smiles and exuberant movements, sweeping me up in her enthusiasm. She physically swung me up from the table and into her arms, even going so far as to pull me into a hard but chaste kiss. I'd emailed her that morning, asking her over at some point soon. I hadn't expected 'soon' to be just an hour later. It was only ten in the morning.

I chuckled as she dropped into the chair she'd pulled me from. "What's made you so happy?" I lowered myself into the seat next to her with much more grace.

She leaned back, her glowing smile relaxing into something content. She looked good. Joy had always suited her. It lit up her entire face, somehow making her even more beautiful than she already was. The light jacket over a crisp shirt tucked into blue jeans helped. She'd always had a way with clothes. I'd equal parts envied it and drooled over it the entire time I'd known her.

She waved a lazy hand. "Several things. We lost the hunters, and the others have agreed to move on to a country none of us have any ties to, so we can finally relax a little. The others have been stressed to the point we haven't done much botany studies. On a better note, they have all started showing much better control over their bloodlust. I know it's a long journey, but they're all doing really well."

An uphill battle for every vampire, but one that was all the sweeter once one established true control. I distinctly remembered the first time I was able to get a handle on my bloodlust. It felt like I was finally gaining some semblance of life back, instead of being constantly driven by hunger.

"Congratulations. No doubt it's you're impeccable teaching."

"You got that right," Colette laughed. It was difficult, even after all this time apart, even with my infatuation with Saira, not to be caught in Colette's gravity. I'd once wrote a poem about her—yes, I'd gone through a poetry phase, and yes, I'd written numerous poems about Colette, we all have our cliché moments, it's not nice to judge people—comparing her to the first whisper of a summer breeze, to the sun peaking over the horizon after a long, cold night, to the last breath before lips touch. Of things to look forward to and anticipate. She was inevitable in a way I'd never experienced with anything else before.

I'd always loved when she became overcome with passion. It ignited a glow within her, from the way she gesticulated more in excitement, to the way she held herself with more certainty, to the way her eyes held a raging fire I threw myself in each time.

It was a struggle stopping myself from getting caught up in her happiness. I'd called her here for a dire reason, after all.

"My stomach is full," she continued, resting her hands over said body part. "I won't need to feed again for a good five or six months, at least."

"I'm jealous," I groaned, barely resisting the urge to bang my head against the table. Spike Man and the four hunters hadn't made much of a dent in my hunger.

Sympathy sat in the tilt of Colette's head. "You always were too picky." She threw her hands up against the glare I sent her way. "Don't worry, your morals are still rubbing off on me. I fed on, in no particular order, a man stalking his coworker, a couple who preyed on the elderly and stole their money, and an entire group of fifteen people running an underground puppy mill." She shook her head, anger throwing joy from her face. "I made sure the dogs are going to be looked after in good homes."

Colette liked to bitch and moan about the so-called morals I'd pushed on her, but she was a massive animal lover who would gladly tear through anyone hurting any animal and not lose a wink of sleep over it. If anything, she was as picky as I was. Maybe it had been *her* who'd pushed her morals onto *me*. It had been so long I honestly couldn't recall.

I blew out a breath. "I wish I could find an underground puppy mill and feed on everyone there." On cue, my stomach growled.

Colette rolled her eyes. "Don't wish a puppy mill on the puppies. Why don't I help you find people? I know you asked me over here, but

I'm glad you did. We're leaving for England soon, then onto someplace warmer for the winter. I was thinking Italy, or maybe Greece if you want, as you love it so much. Your Greek and Italian still as sharp as ever? How about your Neapolitan? Sicilian?" She raised an eyebrow, a cheeky grin spreading over her face. I was fine with Italian, but after the Unification of Italy I never spoke any of the other languages with any frequency and had lost most of them. My Neapolitan was dreadful. "What do you say?"

Hope burned in her eyes, clear as day. We knew one another too well to mask our emotions. What I couldn't quite ascertain was if she wanted to travel with me as a friend or pick up our romantic relationship again. I hadn't sensed any non-platonic feelings from her at the Gardens, but that could have changed after catching up again. Feelings were fickle like that.

"That's actually why I asked you over," I said, picking at the sleeve of the lovely black jumper Michaela had bought for me. It was as comfortable as it looked. Michaela herself was supposed to be here for this extremely important conversation, but she'd left earlier citing some issue with her business. One of the first things I'd taught her—and I used the word taught very loosely, as she already had an extensive background in economics and business—was to set up financial ventures in whichever city she planned to stay in for a while. It was less important to me, as I had more than enough money to fall back on, but she was young and needed to build her cushion. She'd done well on that front this past year. That side of mentoring had been really easy, considering she probably knew more about money and finance than I did.

"You do want to come with me?"

Eagerness laced Colette's words, and to be honest, I didn't know how I felt about it. I would always love Colette, that went without saying, and while we'd both had intense relationships with other people throughout our lives, we did always come back to one another. Inevitable, like I'd mentioned. But I couldn't deny the hold Saira had over me. She was who I wanted.

"It's not that," I said carefully, before ploughing on ahead. Colette had always appreciated bluntness. "The hunters have us all on file. I intend to break into the guild and erase those files, so we can live our lives a little easier. I asked you here to see if *you'd* want to join *me*."

The ticking of a clock filled the room, each second the bang of a drum made louder by the lack of any other sound. Gone was Colette's carefree happiness, replaced by a tension that held her body rigid. I wanted to smooth my hands over her shoulders, to rub that stress away. I hated that I was the cause, but those records *needed* to be destroyed.

"Why not ask Saira to erase them for you?"

Colette's tone was neutral, closed off.

I'd messaged Saira as soon as I'd woken up, but still had no answer. I hoped she was okay. Who knew what damage Sam had been able to inflict before I'd gotten to her.

"I will, but in the event she can't, will you come with me? The others with you, too? You're all on file. They know your names, faces. It'll be better for all of us if they were permanently erased."

I injected as much urgency into my voice as I could, but Colette remained unmoved. Outwardly, at least. The thumb of her right hand had started tapping against the table, the snare to the clocks hi-hat.

"Do you remember our time in Southern Spain, whiling the days away in that villa the old group bought?" Colette's eyes held mine, her intense gaze at odds with her soft voice, the sound broken only by the rhythmic off beat of her thumb and that annoying clock. "Sun baked and blood soaked. You looked radiant, as always. Hot weather agrees with you, and you agree with hot weather." A smile, fleeting. "I remember a particularly sunny afternoon; I was lounging on the deck, and you were in the pool. I remember the way the sun made the water sparkle, like it was shining just for you. Everything was glistening, shimmering, anything felt possible, and you were there in the centre of it all. Beautiful. I remember you smiling up at me and I thought: yeah, I would gladly follow you anywhere. Spend eternity by your side. I don't know if I'm wearing nostalgic glasses, but I think they were simpler days. Better days, some could argue.

"Now you want us to storm a hunters guild and probably die because your latest crush can't do the job herself?"

I blinked at the harsh words and harsher tone. A frown pulled Colette's brows together, pinching her face. Looking at her, it was like she'd never been joyful and relaxed in her life.

"I don't understand why you seem... jealous?" I said, the words coming out as a question. Because that's what it looked like, didn't it? Jealousy? Except Colette wouldn't know jealousy if it walked up to her and shoved a stake through her heart. Which didn't kill us, by the way. Humans were quite inventive in their stupidity. I mean, a glorified stick, really? "We've both been infatuated with a lot of other people over the centuries," I went on. "Why is Saira the one to piss you off now ?"

Colette sighed. "I know, Anna, that's not... I know eternity is a very long time, and I know we have had and will have amorous feelings for others. Hell, Saira's hot. *Really* attractive. If she wasn't a hunter, I'd suggest a ménage à trois. But she *is*. I'm not jealous, Anna, I'm *scared*. I don't want you to get hurt, or fucking *killed*."

I reached over and pulled her hand to my lips, kissing that dancing digit. I kissed each knuckle until I felt some of the stiffness leave her body, and even then, I kept her hand clasped in both of mine. "Maybe we won't have to 'storm the guild' as you so dramatically put it," I said, hoping to add a touch of humour to the conversation. "I'll ask Saira first. I think she'll try. She might even succeed; in which case all of this worrying is for nothing. Okay? Can you try not to stress until I know if she can or not?"

Colette squeezed my hands. "When will you know?"

"I'll text her, ask to see her tomorrow."

"All right," Colette said, the 'right' trailing off into a sigh. "I suppose if she can't, I'll come with you. I'll try to convince the others, but no guarantees."

"Are you sure?"

"Like I said, I'd follow you anywhere. I know you'd do the same for me if I asked."

I would. In the blink of an eye. I stood and enveloped her in a crushing hug, as if I could pour all of my emotions into her if I pressed hard enough. "Thank you."

She nodded. "I know how much you look over your shoulder," she said, the words whispering through my hair. "Always moving, never staying anywhere for more than a couple of years. It's a hard way to live. And I know with your face on record, you'll be even more paranoid."

I made to protest—I wasn't *paranoid*, thank you very much—but Colette held me tighter. "Yes, you are." I heard the smile on her lips. "It's not being *vigilant* to live the way you do. It's paranoid."

I grumbled but didn't complain. She was right, after all. We pulled back from one another, and I took in Colette's half-smile, the resigned set of her shoulders, the love in her eyes. "Thank you," I said again. "If we have to go in and do it ourselves, I promise I won't let anything happen to you."

She gave me a wry smile. "Don't make promises you can't keep. Remember what happened to Luis and Demir?"

Of course, I did. They'd been part of the 'old group' as Colette had called it. There'd been eight of us, all queer couples, and Colette and I were the only ones left. Luis and Demir had been the last to die, in what would turn out to be the last raid on a hunter's guild. The hunter's technology had been advancing at a frankly disgusting rate, and Luis and Demir, along with three others I hadn't known well, had gone in to find information on some terrifying new darts they had.

Needless to say, no one survived.

"You mean you don't want to go out in a blaze of glory, wrapped in each other's arms as we pass from this mortal coil?"

Colette pulled a face at my sardonic comment. "On that note, I'm leaving to speak to the others. Keep me updated on what Saira says." She paused, a smirk breaking out over her face. "And does." She waggled her eyebrows, prompting me to tut at her. Gone was serious, grim Colette, her playful nature once again making an appearance.

"Honestly, you have such a one-track mind sometimes."

"Oh, you mean you're going to see her and *not* have sex?"

I didn't respond, which was response enough. I didn't tell her I wasn't sure if I'd even get a reply to my message, never mind the chance to physically meet up.

Colette's head tipped back as she laughed. "That's what I thought." She stepped into my space, roses filling my nose, her lips brushing my ear and making me shiver. What was it with women and my ears lately? "Do that thing with your tongue. You know what I mean. It's *very* enjoyable."

With that, she swept around me and out the door, closing it softly behind her. I chuckled at her antics, shaking my head as I went into the living room and sank into my comfy armchair.

Colette was on board. Good. I'd ask Michaela, Colette would ask her new friends, and hopefully we could pull it off. Hopefully we wouldn't have to in the first place. As urgent as my appeal had been, and as flippant my response to the memory of Luis and Demir, dread coiled deep in my gut, a snake ready to lash out at anything. I didn't want to break into a guild. I didn't want to put Colette anywhere remotely near danger. But I *couldn't* stay on hunter's records. I couldn't let her stay on them either. I. Just. Couldn't.

Picking up my phone, I messaged Saira again.

10

Saira finally responded after eight agonising hours. I spent the time futilely attempting to read, and when that didn't work, I researched the richest bastards living in Dublin. It would be good to feed on them. I passively acquired wealth after centuries and donated a lot, but they horded it, stole it, and generally made the world and people's lives more difficult for it. We weren't the same. No. The aristocracy could burn for all I cared. I'd go back to my roots, like I had with the Beyer corporation, and kill rich arseholes. Four businessmen had caught my eye and were in Dublin for their biannual 'men only' get together. The day flew by as I investigated them, their businesses, and their movements. They seemed like easy pickings.

The hotel Saira's message told me to meet her at was one of the better ones, to my surprise. I didn't know what kind of budget Saira had brought to Ireland, but it was enough to splash out on a room at a high-end hotel. Did she just want to talk, or would I get to experience the luxurious beds first hand?

I made my way up to room 215 and knocked. The door opened a few seconds later, Saira yanking me unceremoniously over the threshold without so much as a hello. Excitement made my body tingle until I clocked the frown on her face. Thunderous skies looked calmer.

"Were you followed?" she asked as she paced the large room. I briefly glanced around—cream walls, dark furniture, bed pride of place against the wall to my right—but Saira demanded my attention.

"No," I said, my body tingling from agitation instead of excitement now. "What's happened?"

Saira stopped pacing and tilted her head up to the ceiling. Her hair was mussed, like she'd ran her hands though it over and over. She wore black joggers with a rather unflattering baggy black t-shirt, nothing special, and I once again felt overdressed as I removed my coat and threw it over the sofa. I'd chosen blue jeans paired with a white silk shirt.

"What happened to Sam?" She answered my question with one of her own.

"I killed her."

Saira deflated, her head dropping to face the floor and her hands balling into fists. "I thought so." She looked at me for the first time since I arrived. "Why?"

I shrugged. "I followed you both to the guild. Waited for a bit, not really sure what to do. I was going to leave when I saw her leave with three others. I followed them, intercepted them, and killed them." I took a step forward, holding my hands up, imploring her to trust me. "You know she didn't believe you, right? She asked me when I'd turned you into a vampire, asked how many guild secrets you'd told me. Killing her was an act of self-preservation, really. She said she'd put me in the database, registered me as high priority. Said I'd compromised the guild."

My voice rose in a question. Saira ignored it, instead dropping onto the end of the bed, looking as tired as I'd ever seen her. "I've spent most of today in interrogation. I'd called you an informant, not expecting anyone to look into it. Next thing I know, I'm getting dragged out of bed and grilled about how I'd missed you were a vampire." She rubbed a hand down her face. "Then Sam and the others were officially logged as missing. The whole guild is on high alert. You're suspect number one."

I leaned against the back of the sofa opposite her, my body feeling heavy. That had to mean most, if not all, of the hunters knew my face. Erasing the information and as many hunters in the guild had been important before, now it was a dire need. I almost laughed. What a joke my life had so quickly become.

"How are you here?" I asked. Anything to stop my mind from spiralling. "I take it you managed to convince them of whatever story you made up?"

"Yeah," Saira sighed. "Took a long time, and I've probably forever damaged my ego and reputation, but yeah."

I wanted to know what she'd said but held my tongue. Not only did she seem weary, but there was also an anger simmering below her surface, and I didn't want to make it boil over.

"Sam was my friend, y'know?" Saira said, a sadness bubbling right alongside that anger. "Before all this shit happened. As much as I can be friends with the people under my command, anyway."

"For what it's worth, I'm sorry. It genuinely was self-defence." I was limited in my capacity to care about a dead hunter who'd attacked me and was currently ruining my life from beyond the grave, but I *was* apologetic I'd caused Saira pain. I'd never wanted that.

Saira as she abruptly stood, her beautiful brown eyes searing my own. "Ever since I met you, you've fucked everything up for me." Her voice was low, a velvet growl, as she advanced on me. Goosebumps erupted along my arms. If I didn't know any better, I'd think she was going to pull out a gun and hand me over to the guild. "Sometimes I wish I'd never been assigned the Beyer job. Or that you'd never shown up here. Sometimes I wish I could go back to living in black and white, vampire bad, hunter good, and not question fucking everything." She stopped right in front of me. I barely heard her whispered words over the wild drumming of her heart. "Why did you have to turn my world upside down?"

"Would you really be content in ignorance?"

I held my breath, and she held hers. The world paused, both of us balanced on a precipice, and someone falling was only a matter of seconds.

Saira's exhale hit my lips a moment before her own did. She grabbed my shirt and tugged me flush against her body, her tongue demanding entry. I steadied myself with hands on her hips and gladly opened to her. She was hard and rough and wanting, taking and taking, and I grew dizzy with arousal. She'd liked it hard at the retreat, but I wouldn't have said we'd been rough with one another then, not like she was being now. I found myself submitting before her, willing her on as she bit down on my lower lip and ran a soothing tongue along the indentations her teeth had no doubt left.

A groan caught in the back of my throat, quickly stifled as her mouth came down on mine again. I wrapped my arms around her waist, more to keep myself anchored than anything else, and her hands dived into my hair, pinning my head in place as she kissed me to within an inch of life. She tasted of desire, hot and smouldering, like we were moments away from going up in smoke. I grew heady with want, and my stomach clenched as Saira relaxed her hands in my hair, instead choosing to let them fall, one to my neck, the other to a breast.

Both hands squeezed, and a moan stuttered in my throat. She couldn't *actually* hurt me—humans didn't have the strength to strangle us with their bare hands—so instead of feeling constrained, another pulse of arousal beat through me.

My own hands tightened on her hips, and I had to consciously relax my grip. She couldn't hurt me, but I could hurt her. I wanted to give her pleasure, not pain. Sliding my hands from her waist to her arse, I dug my fingers into the soft swell of muscle. Saira's breath hitched, and she dropped both hands to my shirt, unsteadily undoing the buttons as she peppered my neck with open mouthed kisses. I let my head fall back to give her more space.

She yanked my shirt off as soon as she opened all the buttons, and the brief rush of cool air did nothing to calm my overheated skin. Saira moved down from my neck to my collar bones to the tops of my breasts, roughly palming them as she kissed and nipped and sucked, and I buried my hands in her hair to keep her on my chest.

That, unfortunately, had the opposite effect.

She straightened and spun us around, walking me backwards to the bed. Her eyes were a dark haze of want and anger and need and other things that flashed by too quickly for me to focus on, and unease stirred in my gut.

I stopped in the middle of the room. She continued pushing for a moment before she realised she was nowhere near as strong as me, and frowned at my immobility.

"Are you okay?" I asked softly. I needed her to want this, want *me*, not need some kind of random release from the stress she'd been under lately.

She blinked at me, some of that haze clearing from her blown pupils.

"Do you want this?" I asked when she didn't answer.

Her hands, which had been gripping my shoulders, smoothed down my arms and slipped into my own. She interlocked our fingers and leaned our foreheads together.

"Yes," she said, her voice barely a whisper. "I'm sorry. If you want me to slow down or stop I will, I just, I—" she closed her eyes and sucked in a deep breath. "Sorry. I want you. I do. I just need…"

I knew what she was trying to say. She was angry and scared and wound up, and she needed to let it out. I nodded. "You can't hurt me. It's okay. If you want to fuck me hard, go right ahead."

After all, we had all night. She could get the stress out of her system early, then we could move onto more sensual love making. Anyone could have a quick fuck, but I liked to make sure I was remembered. I liked to take my time, memorise my lover's body throughout the night, making sure I knew every way to satisfy her. If that was fast and rough, fair enough. I did like that, but for me, nothing beat slowly pulling the pleasure out of your partner with deep kisses and firm, lingering touches. That slow build up, the panting and pleading as you worshiped her body, the taste of her desire, the rush of her arousal until, finally, all the tension snapped in an intense, exquisite moment.

I had to take a deep breath.

Saira dropped my hands and took a small step back, reaching up and whipping her large t-shirt off in one smooth motion. Smooth skin revealed itself to my starved eyes, and I drank in the flat plains of her stomach, the slope of her breasts, before she was back on me, jerking our hips together as she bit down on my neck.

A breathy laugh rushed out of me. Her answering smile tickled my skin as she licked over the troubled area. "Couldn't resist," she said, then no more words were exchanged as she kissed me hard and deep, leaving me reeling, desire clouding up my head and tightening my stomach. I needed her on me right that second.

We pulled the clothes off one another as fast as we could, an urgency taking hold. She shoved me backwards onto the bed, immediately following and stretching her naked body over mine. The heat of her skin set me on fire, and the smell of her apricot shampoo and her arousal and her blood and *her* was enough to have me seeing stars, and we'd barely done more than make out and get a bit handsy.

Speaking of hands, Saira's were pushing my legs apart. She gave me one last kiss, nipping my lower lip, and pulled back. I let my eyes slide shut and head flop back onto the pillows, anticipating the first touch of her tongue.

It never came.

Instead, she threw a leg over one of mine and aligned our centres, pulling my other leg up her body. I had a second to think *fuck yeah*, then her pussy came down on mine and she started grinding us together. Fast. Hard. Her breasts bounced with each thrust of her body and all I could do was cling to the bed sheets as she moved relentlessly.

I knew tribbing didn't work for some women, but it did for me. And it clearly did for Saira. I watched her above me, her body a beautiful work of art, all soft curves and smooth movements and loud gasps, and felt my pleasure building. Her hair fell down her back as she tilted her head, her fingers digging into my thighs as she moved even faster. If I'd been human, I had no doubt her touch would have bruised.

The bed sheets tore under my hands, but I couldn't have given less of a fuck. Both mine and Saira's moans filled the room, and my body grew more and more tense, more and more tight, until everything came apart. My orgasm rushed through me like a maelstrom, rapid and powerful, and my body felt rigid and loose at the same time.

"Fuck, *Saira*." The words slipped past my lips as I rode out my orgasm, and she grinned down at me, not slowing in the slightest.

A sheen of sweat covered her body, giving her an otherworldly, ethereal look. I'd come quickly, I knew that, but how was she still going? Her pace was *brutal*.

I fucking loved it.

My pleasure began to crest again, but before it could build back to maelstrom levels, Saira's movements lost their fluidity. Her eyes slammed shut as her body jerked against mine, and she let out a long groan. Her expression twisted like she was in pain, but that was how Saira wore her pleasure.

So beautiful.

Her erratic thrusts slowed to a stop, and she collapsed on top of me, panting and sweaty and magnificent. I held her close and planted kisses along her jaw as she collected herself. I tried to deepen the moment, but she pulled away and rolled off me.

"Is everything okay?" I asked, wondering for the first time if sleeping together had been a mistake. Unease cooled some of my desire. I didn't want to be just a warm body to help her forget her problems. She mattered to me; I wanted to mean something to her too. The thought of wrapping myself up in the covers to shield myself from her silence flashed through my mind, but I didn't entertain the idea.

Instead, I propped myself up on an elbow. Communication was key to any kind of relationship, and she wasn't going to get away with freezing me out.

"Saira? Talk to me."

She scrubbed a hand over her face. "Sorry. I've kinda ruined the moment, haven't I?" She gave a self-deprecating laugh, and I soothed a hand over her stomach, silently urging her to get whatever was bothering her off her chest.

"I was..." she paused, shaking her head. She frowned at nothing for a few seconds. I let her gather her thoughts. She abruptly met my gaze, the brown of her eyes dark and stormy, and she laced our hands together on her stomach. "I thought coming here, seeing you, fucking you, would get you out of my system. I'm under so much pressure to find you and bring you in. But you've made everything so *complicated*. You make me so confused. I don't know whether I want to kiss you or turn you in or take you on a fucking date from one minute to the next, and I feel like my head will never stop spinning."

My breathing threatened to grow ragged. All this time, I'd assumed she liked me the same way as I liked her; letting my feelings take the lead, regardless of our differences. But it seemed she was more conflicted about us than I'd realised.

"I'm so angry all of the time," she continued, her thumb rubbing softly over mine. "Y'know, vampires killed my entire family. My parents were the only survivors, fleeing to America to escape. They assimilated totally into American culture. Well," she stopped, a small smile curving her lips. "Apart from the food. Mom couldn't bring herself to leave that behind as well as everything else." She sighed. "I get it. They were running from their trauma, both physically and metaphorically, but I don't know." Saira stopped again, her gaze dropping from mine, her lashes resting against the curve of her cheek. "Is it possible to miss something you've never had?"

When her eyes met mine again, a vulnerability startled me. I fought the urge to wrap her in my arms and protect her from all the horrors of the world.

Instead, I simply nodded.

"I miss my family," Saira said. "Aunts and uncles and cousins and grandparents who were killed before I was born. I miss the culture I should have been brought up in. I can speak some Urdu, but I can't read or write it. My parents never taught me, and I never asked. By the time I was old enough to get my head out of my ass and ask about their culture and why they left Pakistan, I became consumed with vampires and hunting as many as I could." She let go of my hand and started drawing random patterns up and down my arm. I splayed my fingers over her stomach, keeping my touch as light as hers. Letting her know I was listening to what she had to say.

"Y'know, I'm quite unusual in hunter circles." She gave a little shake of her head. "Most are born into it; that's the most common type of hunter. A lot have family or friends murdered by vamps and get into it when hunters come to clean up the mess. I'm unusual in that I sought them out after my parents told me everything. My parents are worried sick all the time, but I always come home. Always. I know they wish they'd never told me anyway."

She stopped abruptly. The silence filling the space her soft words had occupied felt oppressive, uncomfortable. I'd known hunters seemed to have personal stakes in killing us, and while I'd always suspected the reason, it was wholly different hearing it spoken out loud. I knew I wasn't a saint. I knew my kind killed to live. I knew we tore families apart. But we never stayed around long enough to witness the aftermath, so the knowledge had remained abstract. I searched within myself and found a faint stirring of guilt. But as I focused on it, that's all it remained: faint. I would never apologise for surviving. The best I could do was what I was already doing, feeding on bastards and predators.

Saira sighed into the quiet. "Point is, I'm angry. I have been since I found out about everything. And for the most part, vampires were the perfect target for all my fury. We're taught that you murder innocent people indiscriminately, that you all need to be eradicated like some horrible disease. I believed that for a very long time. Then you came into my life, with your 'I try to kill bad people' and 'the world isn't black and white' and 'humans can be just as bad'." Saira's hand didn't stop it's slow meandering along my arm, the soft movement at odds with her harsh words. "You've thrown my entire world view into a tailspin, and I'm so *confused*."

I shuffled a little closer to her, keeping one hand on her stomach and running the other through her hair. "Your rage isn't wrong," I said. "The vampire who turned me also killed my family. I was angry for a long time. *So* angry. But I've also been around for a long time and have come to terms with the world. Some people, vampire and human alike, are just awful. There are a lot of nuances to it, bad childhood, some kind of trauma, I don't know. They do horrible things and enjoy them. But the opposite is also true, again, for vampire and human alike. I once had a friend who tried to feed on animals to avoid killing humans. Didn't work, human blood is the only type that sustains us, but she tried. She became a vet, dedicating her life to rehabilitating injured animals. I know she always felt guilty about trying to feed on them. She was a lovely woman. One of the kindest people I've ever met. Hunters found and killed her."

Her name had been Caroline, and I'd been remiss in not remembering her for a while. I'd lost so many friends over the years it was difficult to keep their memories alive.

"And you know the bloodlust cools as we age," I continued, threading my fingers through Saira's hair. She gazed up at me, the anger in her eyes long since evaporated, leaving behind a tired kind of acceptance. "But when we're first turned it's horrendous. Does that make young vampires evil, or are they simply not in control? If more lived to be my age, they would be able to plan more, perhaps do as I do and target a certain type of person." I brought the hand that had been resting on Saira's stomach up to caress her face.

"I don't know what the answer is," I said, my voice soft in this bubble we'd carved for ourselves, "but I know hatred isn't it. All that leads to is a cycle of more violence. I hated every hunter for centuries, and then I met you. You've reminded me that nuance exists in every person, in every situation, and that perhaps I shouldn't blindly despise you all." I chuckled under my breath. "Easier said than done, of course. Hunters have hurt me a million times over, and I don't forgive easily."

No matter what I said, I didn't think I could ever fully let go of the loathing that had settled in my bones over the centuries, growing with me as I aged. Believing there were more hunters like Saira, who saw we weren't mindless killing machines, was nice, and I could tell she wanted to believe the same of vampires, but it was probably more fantasy than reality. I didn't have the answers to the war that had been waging between us since time immemorial. Vampires would always need to feed, and humans would always take issue with that.

Saira brought her hand up to my face, mirroring my caress. "What a shitty mess we're in." We both laughed. "I'm supposed to bring you in, but I've never seen you, okay?"

I smiled down at her. "Okay."

She pulled me down, our lips meeting in one of the softest kisses I'd ever had. Gone was the angry, rough Saira, and in her place was a woman so gentle it almost brought a tear to my eye. I stopped her before she could deepen the kiss.

"What is it?"

"At the risk of ruining this very beautiful moment, I have to ask." I paused, and the frown on her face grew more prominent the longer I didn't speak.

"Anna?"

I pursed my lips. "Can you erase me from the hunter database? I'm sorry to ask, I know it will probably be horribly dangerous for you—"

"No."

"No as is it won't be dangerous or no as in—"

"No as in I can't remove you from the database."

Oh. I deflated, feeling fear settle itself across my shoulders. It seemed storming a guild was in my future. *Fantastic.* I'd done a lot in my time, mastered a lot of skills, climbed to the top of many professions. I was *good* at what I put my mind to. I had faith in my own competence.

But I'd never infiltrated a hunter's guild before, and that shit was terrifying. One slip up, one missed dart, and I was dead.

"I'm sorry," Saira said. She did look genuinely apologetic. "Not only is the risk of capture too high, but I'm here as a guest. I don't have the clearance and I wouldn't know where to start if I did. And I'm pretty sure I'm under surveillance. Definitely inside the guild. I think had to shake a tail to get here, but to be honest it was so easy I'm not sure it was a tail at all."

I frowned at her. "Are you safe there?"

She shrugged. "Yeah. My story of being a poor, sad lesbian seduced by an outrageously gorgeous woman is pretty solid. They think you got close to me to get insider information on the guild. Gave me some information so I'd give you some. When I told them we mainly fucked, most of them got uncomfortable. Luke was so disgusted he left the room." She rolled her eyes. "Never thought homophobia would save my ass." I chuckled at her sarcasm. "They'll keep me under observation for a while, but I convinced them I hadn't given you anything significant. I can kiss having a team goodbye, though. I've been compromised, and there's no coming back from that, especially with my already suspicious history."

I continued stroking my hand through her hair. "I'm sorry. I really have fucked your life up, huh."

"I'll be fine. You on the other hand." She gave me a little shove. "*You* need to leave the city. The country."

I shook my head. "I'll think of something. I can't leave knowing they have my details."

"Speaking of details," Saira said, a soft sigh escaping her lips. "I'll be out all night. That's suspicious. Can you give me anything? I can say I was out looking for the botanists or something, because I'm so desperate to get back in the good books." Again, her sarcasm made me chuckle.

"I'll message Colette and ask for the address. She'll move everyone before the hunters show up."

Saira nodded. "Thanks."

"You don't have to thank me for helping keep you safe. But let's not think of that right now. Let's have the rest of this night, then we can go back to reality in the morning."

She stared at me for a long moment, her gaze bouncing between my eyes, before she nodded.

"Tonight."

"Tonight," I repeated, and captured her lips once more. She immediately opened to me, pulling me fully on top of her and palming my breasts. I let myself get lost in her body, in her smell, in the sounds tearing themselves from her throat, making sure I coaxed every last drop of pleasure from her until the early hours of the morning.

I refused to think about what I'd have to do. We had the night, and Saira was all that mattered.

11

We followed the four businessmen all day. They met around lunch time at a golf course and stayed there for hours. Golf had always bored me to tears, and that afternoon was no exception. Crazy golf was fun, but actual golf? No thanks. I would rather have spent the day watching paint dry, but my growling stomach had other ideas. As much as I wanted to knuckle down with Colette and figure out a way to rid the Dublin guild from the world, in that moment, I needed blood more.

As the daylight died the four men drove to the house they'd rented for the week. Their 'men only' get together was an excuse to ditch their responsibilities, get drunk and high, and potentially cheat on their wives. All four had met at university, and they were shitty people with even shittier business practices. Two dealt in the pharmaceutical industry, one in food, one in clothing. All lied, all cheated, all underpaid workers almost to slavery. In the case of Darren, the one in clothing, actual slavery happened in the production line.

Disgusting. I couldn't wait to feed on them all.

Well, on half. Michaela also needed blood.

We stood shrouded in shadow, careful not to let the light spilling from the windows of the house reach us. The sprawling residence was remote—rich people didn't like rubbing shoulders with the common folk—which played right into mine and Michaela's hands.

I had to stop myself from bouncing on the balls of my feet. Excitement made me want to *move*, and I had trouble reigning the impulse in. Michaela had no such qualms. She shifted her weight from foot to foot like she was warming up to run a race.

"Okay," I said, my breath misting in front of me. Ugh, I really hated the cold. "When we go in, I know all you'll want to do is tear into the first one you reach, but I want you to knock him out then grab the second one to feed on first. If you get lost in the bloodlust the others have a chance to get away."

Michaela nodded. "I'll be able to do it this time. I will."

"I know you can."

Michaela had been an exceptional student, internalising my lessons quickly and with little repetition. That being said, she still struggled to control herself around blood. I had every faith in her—she truly was a gifted woman—she just needed to believe it herself. If she was going to help me infiltrate the hunter's guild, she *needed* to have better control over herself. She wasn't coming with me if she failed here. I wouldn't put her at risk like that.

"After you," I said.

Michaela sucked in a deep breath and barged through the front door like a force of nature, knocking it clean off its hinges and diving straight for Mark, one of the arseholes in the pharmaceutical industry. I followed more sedately, readying myself to catch anyone who tried to run if the bloodlust dug its claws into Michaela.

I need not have worried. Michaela smashed Mark's head off the marble top of the kitchen island, and he crumpled to the floor like a puppet whose strings had been cut. She paused for a heartbeat over the blood oozing from the crack in his skull, but she pulled herself away and dived on Connor, ripping his throat out and guzzling down his blood like there was no tomorrow.

My cheeks hurt from the grin stretched over my face. She'd done it! I'd known she would be able to soon, but it was so *good* seeing her finally exert control. It was a big step for her. Pride radiated out from my chest, warming my entire body. Was this feeling why people mentored others? This potent mixture of happiness and satisfaction? I could have danced for joy.

But it was my turn to feed. The remaining two—Darren and Craig—hadn't moved. Yet another case of freeze over fight or flight and, in all honesty, we were just too quick for them. Maybe five seconds had elapsed at most. How sad for the slow, clumsy humans.

I copied Michaela in bashing Craig's head against the kitchen countertop and stepped over him to Darren. Calling him weasel-faced was an insult to weasels, but it best described his narrow little head and watery eyes. The man was clearly drunker than drunk, which meant his blood wouldn't be the best, but my void of a stomach didn't care. I tore into him with little ceremony and drained him as fast as I could, quickly followed by Craig. And that was that. My hunger felt ever more sated.

I leaned against the counter, wiping excess blood from my chin and licking it off my fingers. Nothing wasted. A few spots marred the black hoodie I'd thrown on, but they weren't noticeable. Michaela copied my stance as she also cleaned herself up.

"I did it." She grinned at me, her smile as wide as the ocean. It was a beautiful sight. *Women are amazing.*

I beamed back at her, delighted she'd taken the next step towards true control. "Well done. You've been getting closer each time we've fed, it was only a matter of time." It was true; she'd kept herself from giving in a little longer the past few times she'd fed. Tonight felt expected. Not to take away from her achievement, of course, just that she was always going to succeed.

"It doesn't feel real," she sighed, gazing down at the four dead men. "I wanted to feed on him, but I was able to blot out the need for long enough to get the other guy too. I knew I'd get to this point, you and the other older vampires are proof of that, but it felt so far away."

I nodded. "For me, too."

She looked up at me. "Really? You can remember?"

The scepticism in her voice made me smile. "I know it was a long time ago, but yeah. That bloodlust isn't something you forget in a hurry, even after five hundred years."

As always, whenever I mentioned my age, Michaela got a faraway look in her eye. "I can't wait until I've been alive that long."

"Really? You've never mentioned it."

My dry tone made her roll her eyes. "Yeah, yeah, I know. Doesn't immortality fascinate you, though? It's part of the reason I said yes to Thomas when he asked if I wanted to be turned. Imagine all the things we're going to see, all the things we're going to live through. All that *change*. I can't wait."

I'd heard it all from her before. She seemed oddly obsessed with living forever, like it wasn't a bit of a chore sometimes. Never mind. She'd find out in her own time.

"What do you think the world will look like in another five hundred years?" she asked. "Hell, just another hundred? I wonder how the political landscape will change."

"The world is in constant flux," I said, shrugging. "Who knows. All we need to concern ourselves with is feeding without getting caught and killed. You can become a scholar of history if you want, but *not* a participant in it. Leave that to the humans. If they discover we're real and not just some folktale used in horror films, I imagine we'll be wiped out pretty quickly."

Michaela pursed her lips, her brows pulling down. "Why haven't hunters gone public? I think you're right; we'd go extinct fast if the world knew."

I shrugged again, rubbing my hands down my black joggers. "You'd have to ask the hunters. My guess is they think they either wouldn't be believed, despite the evidence, or they think it would cause a panic, with neighbour turning on neighbour. It would be the witch trials all over again, but with modern weapons." I shook my head. That had been a ludicrous time. If I thought hard enough, I could still taste the ash on my tongue, still hear the screams ricochet around my ears. I'd tried to save as many as I could. It wasn't enough. Men's hatred of women truly knew no bounds.

Michaela's mouth dropped open. "Were you in Salem during the witch trials?"

"No. Witch hunts took place all over the world. They estimate nine million were killed in Europe alone." It still made me so *angry*, thinking about it. All those women murdered. All the medical knowledge lost or stolen by men. I *hated* it.

"Oh wow. That's *fascinating*. I mean, obviously not that women were killed, but that you've lived through it. I can't wait until I can tell a new vampire what crazy shit I've lived through."

"Let's destroy this guild, and you can."

"Do you think I'm ready? I know I controlled myself this time, but what if I can't the next? Or the time after that?"

I put my hands on her shoulders, brushing invisible lint off a black hoodie identical to mine. "You've done it, which means you can do it again, and again, and again. I won't lie, you will regress sometimes. Blood will always be our Achilles heel, especially if we're hungry, but you've controlled yourself. You know you can do it now." I paused, squeezing her shoulders before dropping my arms back to my sides. "Not to say that it gets *easy*, just that it gets *easier*. I still occasionally struggle, but I haven't lost control for a very long time."

"Okay, that's good." Michaela nodded once, like she was trying to convince herself she'd be fine. "I want to help with the guild, but I wasn't sure…"

I smiled at her. "I know, and thank you again. I don't know how many of Colette's group she'll convince, so it might just be the three of us. Still, if you don't want to or don't feel confident—"

"I want to help," Michaela repeated, her voice not inviting argument. "You've done so much for me. Told me the best ways to get rid of evidence, put me in touch with your contacts in law enforcement and morgues, passed on so much of your knowledge. I'll help. I'd like to think it goes without saying at this point."

She smiled at me, and I felt a little self-conscious. She never had to thank me for any of that. I'd always looked out for my kind, and I'd made the decision to take her under my wing. I'd be a pretty shit teacher if I didn't teach her anything. Every few years some of us worked in various 'jobs of interest', as we called them, in several major cities around the world, to help each other out. Things like doctors in morgues to cover up the lack of blood in bodies. Detectives in law enforcement to mislead investigations into our kills. Of course I'd share that with Michaela.

"Okay," I said, suddenly business-like to cover my strange moment of awkwardness. "Let's see if you've been paying attention." Michaela stood up straight, a small smirk on her face, like she knew what I was doing. "How do we deal with this?" I gestured at the mess around us, the four dead bodies and the damaged door and marble counter.

"They're all drunk and drugged up. We'll damage a bit more of the property, make the police think they got rowdy. And then one of them accidentally started a fire..." Michaela launched into a detailed cover up, and that glow of pride I'd felt since she'd controlled her bloodlust sparked anew.

I remembered my interest in becoming a firefighter then. Neither me nor Michaela had a real job, living off the profits of my sale to the Beyer Corperation and Michaela's savings we'd slid through various fronts, but maybe in the future when we moved somewhere else, I could join a fire station. The itch to try something new wound around my mind like vines, and who didn't like a bit of arson?

Speaking of arson, flames reached twisting fingers into the night sky as we made our way home, our spirits high and our stomachs well on their way to being full.

12

I found myself at the kitchen table for the second time that week, contemplating the culinary arts and how dreadful I would be at them—idly wondering if I could surprise Saira with nihari one day without making myself ill—when Colette let herself in through the back door. I felt caught in a time loop, thrown back to a couple of days ago when I'd asked her to risk her life with me, except this time Michaela leaned against the kitchen counter with her arms folded across her burgundy blouse, and Gracie followed Colette through the door like a little lost puppy.

I waited for more of her botanist friends to appear, but it seemed Gracie was it. Colette saw my face and grimaced.

"The others won't be joining us," she said as she removed her large coat, revealing a shirt and jeans not dissimilar to what she wore the last time she sat in the kitchen, and dropped heavily in the chair next to me. "In fact, they've already left for Belfast. Me giving Saira the house location was too much for them, despite having a backup ready to go." Colette rolled her eyes, letting her wet, windswept hair loose before retying it. Gracie hovered next to Michaela, looking equally as cold and damp as Colette but not removing her heavy coat. It must've started raining.

I balled my hands into fists; the only outward sign of my frustration I let myself express. "They want nothing to do with this insane idea, and I can't blame them," I said. All true; if our positions had been reversed, I would have done the same thing. The whole destroying-the-guild plan, or even just destroying-the-evidence, looked increasingly bleak. Maybe it would be best to cut our losses and leave. Wait for the humans to die. But even then, we were still in their system. Another thought occurred to me, and my stomach sank like a lead balloon. What if the hunters had some kind of global system, like the cloud, where every known vampire was tagged and could be accessed by any hunter at any guild? *Fuck me.* Had the exponential growth of technology slammed the final nail into our coffins? If all it took was a photo that could be shared around the world, there'd be nowhere to hide.

We needed to take down their network. Hack the system. Would Lilli know what to do? The sheer scale of the problem made me want to curl into a hole somewhere and never come out.

I blinked at myself. When had I become so morose? So defeated? I gathered those unhelpful thoughts together, beat them bloody and tossed them aside. I was a five hundred and forty-one year old vampire. I'd seen and done some shit in my time. One measly guild wasn't going to make me roll over and die.

Holding my renewed vigour close to my chest, I stood from the table.

Just as I opened my mouth to start speaking, the front doorbell rang. Everyone frowned. "Are we expecting someone else?" Michaela asked, her back ramrod straight.

"It's okay, I know who it is. One second."

Curious glances chased me from the kitchen to the front door. Saira smiled as I let her in, stomping her boots on the mat and dripping water everywhere. I winced at the mess. If there was one thing I hated more than the cold, it was cold *and* rain.

"Hey," she said, hanging her coat on the hook next to the door and running her hands down her dark grey hoodie. "Do you mind if I leave my boots on?"

I raised an amused eyebrow. "In case you need to make a quick getaway?"

She shrugged, unapologetic. "Yeah. You never know when you might have to start running."

I paused, wondering if I should put shoes on too, before shaking my head at myself. "You really know how to inspire confidence."

Saira grinned and leaned forward for a kiss that was entirely too short. "I like to plan for the worst."

"Come on. Everyone's in the kitchen."

"Anna," Colette said, eying Saira warily as we stepped over the threshold between living room and kitchen. "Why is the hunter here?"

"Saira." Michaela narrowed her eyes.

"Michaela." Saira narrowed hers right back. I belatedly realised I should have warned everyone.

"Not going to shoot me again, are you?"

"You're not going to give me a reason to shoot you, are you?"

The two women had a little standoff, but before I could intervene, they both nodded to one another. *Crisis averted, I guess.*

Saira turned to Gracie. "Not going to try to eat me this time?"

Gracie shook her head at the floor, mumbling something even my heightened hearing didn't pick up.

"I ask again, Anna," Colette drawled, drawing my eyes to her. "Why is she here?" Colette's tone held more curiosity than anger, but I could read between the lines. Her body on the chair had an almost unnatural stiffness to it, with both feet planted on the floor. She looked ready to explode into action. I bit back my sigh because honestly, I couldn't blame her. After everything we've been through together, all the friends we'd lost to hunters, all the roots we'd put down only to dig back up after a few years because hunters moved too close, I understood how difficult it must've been for her to wrap her head around Saira. She *hated* hunters. I did too. I couldn't explain Saira. But that was the nature of feelings, wasn't it? You felt them regardless. They had no laws but their own, and I'd never been one to deny them.

"Saira has kindly gifted us the blueprints to the Dublin guild," I proclaimed, fully expecting the silence that followed. I pursed my lips to stop from grinning like a fool. Who didn't love a dramatic announcement?

"Has she now?" Colette deadpanned, raising an eyebrow first at me, then at Saira. "Well?"

Saira crossed her arms. "You got a laptop?"

I nodded to Michaela, who sighed as she went to retrieve the laptop I'd bought not three hours ago. It was on aeroplane mode. Colette was right, as usual; paranoia had long since taken up residence in my brain and didn't seem like it was going to move out anytime soon.

"And you're doing this out of the goodness of your heart, are you?" Colette said, narrowing her eyes at Saira.

Saira sighed, her entire body deflating as she leaned against the counter opposite Gracie. "I'm so fucking sick of justifying myself to people. Of justifying mine and Anna's relationship." She fixed Colette with a hard stare. "I'm doing this for her. The rest of you are just collateral."

I saw Michaela mouth *'relationship'* as she moved past me, an incredulous slant to her lips, but my attention was held by Saira and Colette. They frowned at one another, and my lungs paused in anticipation of something I couldn't define. Perhaps it was silly of me, but I wanted them to get along. None of my previous lovers had ever caused Colette as much concern as Saira, and Saira, well, she had the potential to become one of the few women I'd ever fallen in love with. I simply wanted them—old, enduring love in Colette and new, thrilling love in Saira—to like each other.

Michaela dropping the laptop on the table broke whatever staring contest Saira and Colette had been having. Colette abruptly grinned. A wide, genuine smile stretched over her face, and I didn't need to look at Saira to sense the confusion wafting from her like heat haze.

"I think you and I are on the same page," Colette said. "We might not be reading the same sentence but we're on the same paragraph, at least. We both want what's best for Anna. You can trust that in me, and I can trust that in you."

"Exactly," Saira agreed, the word stretching out of her mouth. "We both want Anna safe, which means giving you these blueprints." She handed a USB drive to Michaela, who promptly stuck it in the laptop.

"Memorise those as best you can in the next five minutes," Saira said. Both her voice and choice of words seemed suddenly urgent, like the five minutes she'd mentioned were the start of a countdown.

I tore my gaze away from the blueprints and met Saira's eyes. The brown in them looked muddied, tension kicking up a storm and obscuring every other emotion. "What's happened?" I had to force the question through numb lips. She hadn't... she couldn't have...

No. Not Saira. She wouldn't betray me. Something else was going on.

"There's been a change of plan," Saira said. "Hunters are going to storm this house in the next few minutes." Each word was a physical blow. Why would she make such a drastic change in the eleventh hour without telling me?

"What the fuck?" Michaela growled.

Saira held up her hands. "*Listen*, before you all jump to the wrong conclusion—"

"How is you turning us in the wrong conclusion?" Michaela looked ready to throw herself at Saira. I braced myself. We needed to be a coherent unit, *not* jumping down each other's throats.

"Look, you want into the building, this is how it happens." Saira jabbed a finger towards the laptop. "You can get out *much* easier than you can get in." She turned to me, her eyes big and wide, imploring me to understand. "Security has been ramped up since Sam, okay? How do you think I got these blueprints? They gave them to me. They'll come in, tranq you, and take you to the guild. *That's* your way in. The guild is on too high an alert for it to happen your way. And this way, I offer them some vamps, I regain some standing after all the shit that's happened, and you get your chance to erase your files. It's a win-win."

"They won't just kill us here?" Gracie asked, a tremor in her voice.

Saira shook her head. "No, they won't. Can you imagine the clean up? Standard protocol is to tranquilise vampires and move them back to a guild, where they can be... y'know."

Beheaded. Great. I was well aware the majority of plans changed the moment they were implemented, but this was almost a full day before we were supposed to sneak into the guild. I inhaled a large breath in through my nose and released all my shock and stress in an exhale through my mouth. This was happening now. Time to get ready.

Colette and I studied the blueprints as Saira, Michaela, and to a lesser extent, Gracie, argued. It was probably the most I'd heard Gracie speak, which, considering I heard maybe five sentences from her, wasn't saying much.

"You remember Montenegro?" I said to Colette, quiet under the argument.

"When I caught the dart?"

"Exactly. I did the same in the US. We've both done it before so we can both do it again."

"And pretend to be unconscious." Colette nodded once, a firm jolt of her head. "I doubt the darts would wear off before they killed us."

I squeezed Colette's shoulder and turned to Saira, cutting through the fight. "You'll stall them for as long as possible, yeah?"

"Yeah. But try to just fake it, like at the retreat." She held up her hands again as Michaela let out a bitter laugh. "I know this is dangerous. I know a lot can go wrong." Colette let out a faint snort next to me. "Try to catch the darts. Pretend to be unconscious until you get to the extermination room." Extermination room? Really? "If you don't catch them, I'll stall as long as I can. But understand, every hunter knows how long they last, and once it gets into that window there won't be much I can do."

"What is that window, exactly?" I asked. It had taken me ages to wake Michaela at the retreat, but she'd been a walking pin cushion, struck with multiple darts, so I assumed that wasn't an accurate example.

The tendons in Saira's neck stood out for a brief second. "Usually between an hour and an hour and thirty minutes. There have been exceptions over and under, but they're rare. The guys coming in any minute now will want to move fast."

She grabbed my hand and stared into my eyes, her gaze and touch burning, like she'd set my soul on fire. "*Move faster.*"

13

Giving my hand one last squeeze, Saira retreated through the living room and out the front door. I took that as the cue it was and let my senses take over.

Heartbeats, loud like war cries in my ears, surrounded the house. Too many to be the neighbours. Breathing, heavy with anxiety and anticipation and something like eagerness. The occasional muttered sentence or order in a tense whisper. The thick, heady scent of blood that underpinned every sense a vampire had. A rumble shook my stomach. Not feeding on anyone was going to be a chore, but I did *not* want to be caught unawares and catch a dart in my back. I took one more breath in, inhaling the sickly-sweet smell of sweat that lingered around the humans. It curled up my nose like noxious gas, twisting my lip in disgust.

I moved the same moment they burst through both doors.

Five piled into the kitchen like weapon-wielding debris from a tsunami, and I heard four more sweep in through the front door. They wore police riot gear. A good cover, I supposed. They couldn't exactly storm a residential street wearing jeans and a graphic tee.

I dropped my fangs and decorated my face with fear. Not that dread didn't sing in my blood, mind you, I just felt more resolve than terror. I had a dart to catch—probably more than one—and panic didn't make for good reflexes.

I picked up a kitchen chair and threw it at the hunters coming in through the living room. Michaela, Gracie, and Colette were in between me and the five crammed into the kitchen—and honestly, didn't they study tactics at all? What a way to hinder themselves. The ones at the back couldn't get a clean shot, which meant instead of fighting five hunters, the others were fighting two.

I, on the other hand, had four to deal with.

The thrown chair slowed one and incidentally blocked a dart. The hunter didn't have time to recover before I was on them, snapping their wrist so they dropped their weapon and shoving them into the hunter behind. Both tumbled to the floor with shouts, one pained, the other winded. I spared them enough of a glance to clock the second hunter's gun, but the two still standing demanded my attention.

I saw them both squeeze triggers and ducked. Two darts flew over my head and embedded themselves in the wall behind me. I mentally sighed. There went my deposit. The alias I'd used to rent the house would probably end up on some sort of landlord blacklist, if such a thing existed.

Annoyance tainted my resolve, and I grinned at the hunters, baring my teeth at them. A little more fear would do them good. The milky white skin of one went even paler, if that were possible, and the blue eyes of the other widened in alarm. I had a suspended moment of internal laughter at their pathetic displays before both tried to raise their guns again. I didn't give them the chance to lift their arms.

Picking up the chair again, I rammed it into both of them and shoved, sending them and the chair flying through the stair banister.

My deposit was *definitely* gone.

Maybe half a minute had passed. The hunter I'd thrown Broken Wrist on top of finally extracted themselves, and as they were picking themselves up, I chanced a quick glance into the kitchen.

Michaela and Gracie both had darts in their chests. The rush of adrenaline in my veins slowed at the sight, my joy at besting the hunters cooling even as I caught Colette's eye. She winked at me, fake pulling a dart from her neck and falling to the floor, hitting both the table and a cabinet on her way down. I couldn't help but smirk at her antics. If you looked up dramatic, you'd find a picture of Colette.

I whirled on my last hunter to find them already back on their feet and taking aim. My stomach fell off a cliff, and I twisted as they fired, calling on every drop of extra speed and agility my vampirism gifted me.

My fist closed around the dart before it made itself at home in my arm. Heart pounding against my ribs like a convict against the bars of a prison, blood roaring in my ears like the scream of the ocean, I mimed pulling the dart out of my arm as I met the hunter's smiling eyes. They thought they'd got me. *Joke's on you, idiot.* I dropped the dart and fell after it—nowhere near as dramatically as Colette—making sure to land a safe distance away from its poison-soaked tip. The last thing I saw before closing my eyes were thick black boots calmly walking over to me. Hunters were so sure of their superiority. Had they honestly never come across a vampire who only pretended to be unconscious? It had happened to me and Colette twice now, surely others had caught the darts too. Well, I wasn't going to complain too much. Their arrogance worked out well for me.

I kept my features slack as rough hands grabbed me and dragged me out into freezing, heavy rain. I wasn't even wearing shoes. While I lamented my choice not to put any on earlier, whoever was carrying me dropped me onto cold, hard ground, my head smacking against what I assumed was a bench. My hair had been in a loose bun, but half of it had fallen out. The smell of metal and rubber and petrol told me I was in the back of a van.

"Be careful."

Saira. Her voice sounded close. Maybe she was sat on the bench?

"Be careful? Seriously?" A male voice, hard with incredulousness. "She really did a number on you, didn't she. Lesbian sex that good, huh?"

"I found them and led you to them, didn't I? Including her." Saira's voice was a whip, sharp and intense.

The man muttered something that sounded suspiciously like a slur, and I had to make a concentrated effort to keep still. I know I'd said I'd try not to kill anyone so I wasn't too distracted, but that decision went out the window there and then. One less bigot in the world was always a good thing.

The others were dumped in the van next to me. Someone's elbow jabbed me hard in the cheek, and I wasn't able to hide the involuntary grimace. Hopefully no one saw. I didn't hear Saira again, but her smell surrounded me like a cloud, soft and delicate and heavy with promise. Apricots would forever remind me of her. She'd moved to the front of the van while some of the hunters sat on the bench next to us. Only three. There must've been another van.

I kept my body loose as we began driving, even as a boot dug into my hip and that damn elbow jabbed me with every jostle. The hunters—all men, including Mr. Homophobe—laughed and joked about a job well done. Four vamps in one fell swoop. They were going to be legends, apparently. I mentally rolled my eyes so hard a headache began to build.

The drive to the guild wasn't long, but with every horrible word out of the hunter's mouths, it felt like it lasted hours. I was almost looking forward to reaching out destination, just so I could tear them all apart.

14

When the van finally rolled to a stop, I was practically vibrating with the desire to kill them all. It wasn't the fact that they were hunters—although that did play a role in my decision making—it was that I'd been subjected to some of the most degrading commentary I'd ever heard; about myself, about Colette and Michaela and Gracie and Saira, about mine and Saira's relationship, and about women as a whole. Rage pulsed in time with my heart, and staying still was one of the hardest things I'd ever done.

The engine cut. To the hunters, it signalled the end of their mission. To me, it signalled the beginning of the end of their lives. The doors opened, light flooding the gloomy interior, and I made sure I didn't so much as twitch. Two of the three hunters jumped down, one remained standing. The one whose boot had kept such intimate company with my hip, because of course it was.

I let out an even breath. Counted two more heartbeats in addition to the ones already around us. Sound echoed strangely, telling me we were in the garage. From the blueprints I'd studied, the garage wasn't the lowest level. The guild extended a good four floors below the ground.

"Hey, Luke, Brian," Saira said, somewhere off to my left. "We got four."

We were pulled out of the van and dumped onto the hard, concrete floor just as unceremoniously as we'd been thrown into the van earlier. My head smacked against the ground, but all it did was piss me off even more. My hair was all but loose, the hair tie barely hanging on. Losing it would be an annoyance later when I killed and fed on everyone. Getting blood in hair was *not* pleasant. At least nothing was digging into me anymore. Clouds and silver linings, etcetera etcetera.

"Your intel was good." The voice was male, youngish sounding, very Irish, and somewhat surprised, like he hadn't believed Saira. Was he the Luke Saira had mentioned at the hotel? Just how precarious was her position amongst the hunters? I spared a brief thought as to Saira's future after all this. She thought bringing us in would help with her standing, but if she was too burned… Would they hurt her? Would we need to protect her? I understood the benefit of having someone on the inside, so to speak, but not at the expense of her safety. Especially considering this was all a ruse and I was about to kill as many hunters as I could. Would they assume she'd been helping us?

"I already explained everything, Luke," Saira said, sounding exacerbated. "You don't trust me, fine. But trust that I hate vampires just as much as you."

"And yet I've never fuck—"

"Enough."

The new voice was also male, but much older sounding than Luke, gruff and hoarse. Brian, perhaps. Was he in charge?

"Take them to the extermination room immediately," Brian said in a no-nonsense tone. "I want this mess dealt with and put behind us."

Rough hands lifted me from the floor and strapped me into what I assumed was a wheelchair, my head lolling forward and my feet dragging along the floor, then the four of us were pushed into a lift. We went down, two hunters and two wheelchairs per lift, and entered a room than stank so heavily of blood and smoke I was sure the walls were drenched in it. I forced myself to keep breathing despite my body wanting to heave. This was what awaited every vampire caught by hunters. The wonderful smell of blood, tainted by the acrid stench of smoke. Killed, then reduced to ash, all trace of life scoured away. All thoughts, feelings, memories burned into oblivion.

I *hated* them.

We stopped abruptly, the straps chafing against my stomach.

"This place gives me the creeps," the hunter pushing me muttered under his breath. I was inclined to agree.

"Got four for you." The voice wasn't one I recognised. High-pitched and young. A shame, really. He had his whole life to live and instead he became a hunter. Fool.

"Good, good. Help me get them on the tables." Another new voice. I counted seven heartbeats, not including my own or the other vampires. A challenge for Colette and myself, perhaps, but the element of surprise would work in our favour. As soon as they released the straps to move us to the tables, we'd disarm them and revel in their blood. My hungry stomach rumbled the same time a furnace roared to life, and I relaxed my muscles as someone stood over me.

My constraints clicked open.

I launched myself out of the wheelchair, fangs bursting free of my gums and tearing into the man in front of me. He died with shock splashed across his face and I gloried in the taste of hot blood smeared in my mouth.

I didn't loiter, as much as my crying stomach wanted me to. Colette had already killed the hunter pushing her chair and wasted no time diving on another. I spun on the one who'd been pushing Gracie, only to find her fumbling with her gun, which I promptly ripped it out of her hands before she could gather her wits and take aim. She died with a shout, but I wasn't worried. We were quite a way below the main sections of the guild.

With the four hunters dispatched, only the three—what were they called, executioners? Exterminators? Whatever their title, there were only three of them and they carried no weapons. All three looked like the stereotypical serial killer, the kind whose neighbours said they were quiet and nice and kept to themselves in interviews after they'd been caught. Normal looking, but with a peculiarity about them that was difficult to place.

Well, not difficult in this instance. They beheaded vampires and fed us to a furnace for a living. I could think of a few stronger words than peculiar to describe them.

"P-please," one of them stuttered, a redheaded man cringing against a table. "I have a family."

"Really?"

Colette chuckled at the genuine surprise in my voice. I supposed some serial killers did have families. So strange.

He nodded so fast he looked in danger of toppling over. The other two stood frozen, the proverbial deer in headlights, and it occurred to me then that they'd probably never seen a conscious vampire. Cowards, every last one. Who killed unconscious people?

Monsters, that's who. And hunters thought we were the abominations.

Colette nodded at me. "You're the hungry one."

I grinned and advanced quickly, their dying screams echoing in my ears as I killed and fed on them. Glorious blood drenched me, both inside and out, and I finally felt a large portion of my hunger recede, like the tide slowing easing away from the shore. Draining seven people had done wonderful things for my appetite.

"Here." Colette held out my hair tie, which must've given up the ghost during my attack. I took it from her and tied my hair back into a tight bun.

"You couldn't have given me this *before* I got blood everywhere?"

Colette smirked. "That was a sight to behold. And in my defence, I just found it now."

I sent a sceptical hum her way and turned to Michaela and Gracie, both of whom were still slumped in their wheelchairs. "Any idea how to wake them quickly? When Michaela was hit last time it took a while, to say the least."

Colette crossed her arms and frowned down at the two women like they were a complicated equation she couldn't solve. I brought my hands to my hips and glared about the room. We needed to wake them, the sooner the better. No doubt the boss's upstairs were expecting an update about us. I knelt between them, a bloody hand on each knee, and shook.

"Michaela! Gracie! C'mon, wake up!"

Neither moved.

This went on for a good two minutes with no change. My patience rapidly drained away. A sense of urgency curled its way through me, faint at first, but growing in intensity the longer we stayed in that horrific room. The furnace made everything swelter, to the point where even the walls were sweating.

"Wait," Colette said, her voice distant, still partially lost in thought. "What does every vampire crave more than anything?"

"Blood."

"Exactly. Let's see if this works." She coated her hands in blood and shoved them under Michaela's and Gracie's noses, making sure to smear a little over their mouths.

"What, you think we're like cats who wake up when tuna is shoved in their faces?"

Colette laughed. "Worth a shot, right?"

It was worth a shot, because both women twitched awake, Gracie a second or two before Michaela. They awoke so violently, Colette had to snatch her hands away before she lost her fingers.

"Hey, hey, it's okay," I said, trying to calm the frantic women. "We made it into the guild. The plan worked."

"Ready to fuck shit up, or do you need a minute?"

Gracie groaned. "I need blood."

"I second that," Michaela said, clutching her head. "You need to teach me the dart catching trick. They hurt like a motherfucker."

I chuckled. "I think that's something that will come to you with time and experience and not a small amount of luck. But we can certainly train for it."

We gave them another five minutes to gather themselves. I'd never felt the effects of the darts, and looking at the two women struggle not to wince while they walked, even after drinking some of the little blood I'd left, I wanted to keep it that way.

Gracie shed her large coat, her forehead glistening in the heat of the furnace. There was a marked temperature difference near the door, where I hovered, ready to face what lay on the other side. "Colette and I will take the lead. You two follow. Ready?"

Everyone nodded. I sucked in a subtle breath and eased the door open.

Time to destroy a guild.

15

The corridor beyond was empty. As was the next corridor, and the one after that. A barren stretch of white walls and white floors that seemed to go on forever, the monotony occasionally broken by a white door. If I didn't know better, I'd have thought I'd gone colour blind. It was only when we found the stairs and went up a level, did we encounter humans. I let Michaela and Gracie kill the two men in the hope more blood would help wash away the aftereffects of the darts. They did seem a touch more perky with blood in their stomachs.

"What exactly is the plan?" Michaela asked, standing over the broken corpse of the man she'd fed on, the splashes of red a beautiful reprieve from all the white. "We were supposed to sneak in. They know we're here now."

"They think we're currently dead and burning, though," Colette said. "We have some time."

"We head to the armoury, destroy all their weapons and darts," I said, my mind racing through possible outcomes. "They'll figure out we're alive soon, and I think we should minimise the risk of getting shot again." Everyone nodded in agreement. "After that, we'll head to the main operations room. We can access all their files from there, and permanently erase them."

"Risky, but probably the only way we'll get this done." Michaela stretched her neck first to the left, then the right. "A direct assault. Let's do this." Her eyes burned with the same hatred I'd first seen at the retreat, the intervening year doing nothing to dim the flames. Her deep brown irises looked lit from within, giving her gaze a sinister glow. I grinned at her, bloody smile to bloody smile, and felt an answering fury deep in my bones. Hunters had taken so much from all of us. It was time to return the favour.

"Remember," Colette pointed a finger at Gracie and Michaela, "we are stronger, faster, and more agile than the humans. Trust your body, trust your senses, and trust your instincts." She turned to me. "For Luis and Demir?"

"For Luis and Demir." And Caroline and Emílio and Thomas and every other vampire cut down by hunters who saw us as vermin to be exterminated instead of living people with thoughts and feelings and hopes and dreams.

"Follow me."

I lead the way through the maze of corridors, my socked feet flying over the smooth tile as I ran through the blueprints in my mind. The sooner we got to the armoury, the better. The others were silent wraiths behind me, staying close, staying quiet. Our fast progress stalled a few corridors from our destination, partly due to cameras popping up, and partly due to a group of hunters coming towards us. I recognised their voices and anticipation kicked up a storm in my chest. They were chatting about us, the mission, their colleagues broken wrist. I shared a savage grin with Colette.

Instead of glancing around the corner and potentially showing myself, I tuned into my other senses. My eyes fluttered closed, shutting out the bright, artificial light, and my breathing calmed. Eight heartbeats. Boots against tile, but they stepped lighter, like they'd shed their armour. They smelled clean. So, they'd showered and changed, but did they still have their tranquiliser guns? I strained my ears, listening to the noise under their grating chatter, and couldn't hear the tell-tale click of weapons. Which didn't necessarily mean they didn't have any, but I felt a touch more confident. Sometimes, a touch was the difference between life and death.

Their voices were louder, closer. I nodded once to the others, then waited, waited, waited—

I *moved*, an explosion of force and energy the humans had no answer for. I'd tore through three of them before anyone had a chance to react, rejoicing in the smell of blood and fear that sprayed into the corridor. Nothing made me feel more righteous, more powerful, than seeing wicked people cower in terror.

Mr. Homophobe was one such person. I focused on him as the others killed the rest, blood drenching my clothes and arms and face. I knew I was a terrifying sight to behold. The stuff of nightmares, draped in death. Leaning into that image, I bared my fangs as he flattened himself against the wall. His watery blue eyes darted left and right, looking for an escape that wasn't there.

Stepping close, I gripped his neck, slowly squeezing, taking joy from the way his pale face turned a blotchy red. He took a swing at me that I easily caught, and I tutted at him. "Not so big without your gun, are you?" He wrinkled his nose at me. Blood sat heavy on the air. "This is for all the women who have had the misfortune of coming into contact with you, be that passing by in the street, or any girlfriends you've had."

Still pinning his throat, I brought the arm he'd swung up to my face. He started to struggle in earnest, kicking at my legs and clawing at my arm. He made as much an impression as a baby hitting a brick wall. I'd have loved to draw his death out more, but I was aware the others had finished, and there was a camera pointed right at us.

With quick movements, I exposed his brachial artery and drained him quickly. Despite his speedy death, I still found comfort in killing yet another arsehole. The world was a dark and horrible place, but there were rays of sunlight every now and then. His death was one of them.

My stomach rejoiced at all the blood I'd drank so far, and my hunger faded away at a greater rate than earlier. A few more people and I'd be good for another five months or so. As much as I loved feeding, there was something so satisfying about being full. It spoke of a successful feeding spree, of a few less bastards in the world. It meant I could rest and enjoy myself, no more research for a while. I couldn't wait.

Colette broke down the door to the armoury, and the four of us wreaked as much damage as possible. Gracie looked like she was having the time of her life, crushing guns and rifles with gusto. A laugh bubbled in my throat, and I let myself feel the happiness, the freedom, just for a moment. Our actions would not only save us, but lots of other vampires passing through or living in Dublin. If that wasn't worth joy, I didn't know what was.

It didn't take us long to destroy everything. Broken weapons littered the dark floor, empty racks hung from grey walls, and the four of us stood in the middle of it all, grinning at each other. Even if we weren't successful in deleting our files, I still felt a sense of accomplishment. We'd done well. We'd possibly inflicted more damage on the hunters than any vampire had in decades, although I couldn't confirm that. I'd spent years on the move, alone, only connecting with a few friends. No more. I decided, right there in the middle of all the chaos, to spend less time running and more time building a community with my kind. I wanted to help. I wanted to fight back. Looking at Colette and Michaela and Gracie, a feeling like camaraderie stole through me, tying me to them like the Moirai were weaving our destinies together. Colette and I were already braided into a tight twist, but the others knit their way in too.

"They know we're here now," I said, looking at each of them. "You all ready?"

Gracie and Michaela nodded, and a I got a 'hell yeah' from Colette.

"Let's go."

16

The dash to the main operations room was interrupted by a shrill siren and flashing red lights. I clamped my hands over my ears as we all stumbled to a halt. Did they have some kind of special vampire-deterrent alarm? The sound reverberated around my skull and did its best to reduce my brain to mush.

"Is this an anti-vampire alarm?" Colette shouted, giving voice to my own thoughts, her face twisted into an impressive grimace. "Nice of them to announce they know we're coming, at least."

"What do we do?" Gracie yelled, which, well done to her. I wasn't sure she could.

"Stay the course," I said, tentatively removing my hands. The pitch was excruciating, but I wasn't going to let a bunch of sound waves stop me, even if my ears felt like they were bleeding. I wiped my blood-stained hands on my jeans. Unfortunately, there wasn't a way to tell vampire blood from human until you were actually drinking it. The smell was the same from when the vampire had been human, but it didn't taste quite right. Like when milk was on the verge of turning.

I wiped my ears one more time and nodded to everyone. "Let's go."

The rest of the way was unremarkable, bar that fucking alarm. I'd imagined blockages and a small army but was instead greeted by empty corridors and open doors. It didn't feel right. My stomach churned with unease, but the only way out was through.

We stopped around the corner from the main operations room. "We need to prepare if this is a trap."

The others all looked glum, but there was a determination in them too. Steel gazed back at me from three sets of eyes. If there was another fight, they would give it their all. "They might have barricaded the doors. There might be an army of hunters waiting in ambush." The damned alarm blotted out most other sound, so my hearing was out. We were all covered in blood, which hindered my smell, and I couldn't see through walls. We were going in blind. The unease in my gut was well on its way to becoming a category five storm.

"Or," Colette said, a little smile twitching the corner of her mouth up, "they all evacuated and we can delete our information without being interrupted."

I barked out a laugh. "You've always been too optimistic for your own good."

"You both might be right," Michaela said. "They probably have evacuated everyone who isn't field trained, leaving that army of hunters waiting for us."

"Okay, how about this," I said, thinking rapidly. "We break down the doors, if they need breaking down, but don't rush in. They might open fire, and when they stop, *then* we go in."

"Would be better if something went in with the doors," Michaela said. "That way we *know* they'll start shooting."

"I agree," Colette nodded. "I'll go back and get one of the bodies. We can throw that in."

She turned to leave just like that. Like we were out for a causal stroll, and she'd left something behind. I grabbed her arm. "Don't be a brave idiot. What if they're flanking us?"

She clasped our hands together, her eyes boring into mine, the dark blue drawing me in like a rip tide draws unsuspecting swimmers down into the deep. "I'll take Gracie. We'll be back in two minutes, three at most. You can count it, if you want." She squeezed my hand. "I promise. Our story doesn't end here. Besides," she grinned, the blue of her eyes crinkling like sunlight on water, "I need to meet Saira properly, make sure she's good enough for you."

She winked and was gone before I could scoff at her ridiculousness. My unease had graduated to full-blown anxiety. I genuinely felt like I was going to throw up.

A warm hand rubbed my arm. "They'll be okay." Michaela. She smiled at me, and it looked sincere, not like those fake smiles people gave you as false reassurance. "We've made it this far; we'll make it out of here."

I tried to believe her, and a part of me did. All things considered, it had been pretty easy thus far, almost like a guild hadn't been infiltrated for over a century and hunters had grown fat with complacency. Still, overconfidence had been the downfall of many—it wouldn't be mine.

"What's up with you and Colette, anyway?" Michaela asked. "You've got some intense thing going on. I thought you and Saira were a thing?" She held up a hand before I could answer. "Which we are definitely going to talk about when we get out of here. You lied to me about her."

"I did. I'm sorry." I sagged against a wall, the siren still blaring, my stomach still tying itself into knots. "Saira and I... are complicated. Vampire and hunter. Colette and I... are also complicated, I guess. We've been together, on and off, for centuries. That kind of love is lasting. We aren't together at the moment, though, and Saira..." I shrugged. "She intrigues me. She's full of contradictions, and she draws me to her like nothing I've experienced since when I first met Colette. She's quite a masterful liar, but she's also more truthful than most people. She's a hunter and kills our people, but she's protected me several times now, and you all by extension. She's one of the strongest people I know, but I've also seen startling vulnerability from her too. But perhaps that's just an aspect of her strength." After all, it took a lot of bravery to be genuinely open with people.

Michaela hummed. "Is this relationship drama just you, or does it happen to all lesbians?"

I laughed, a soft warmth radiating outward from my chest. We'd grown into good friends in our year of travelling together, and it was nice to joke with her, even in the middle of a guild waiting for either Colette and Gracie to return or hunters to descend on us.

"Hey," I said, the realisation making me chuckle more. "You're the token straight in the group."

Michaela blinked, her laugh matching mine. "I take it Gracie is queer as well?"

"Yeah. Bisexual, so at least you have someone to talk about men with."

She rolled her eyes. "Somehow, I doubt that."

Colette and Gracie chose that moment to return, carrying the body of one of the dead hunters between them. Both grinned as they reached us. My tangled stomach righted itself, relief making my limbs loose. "Told you everything would be fine," Colette said, dropping the body on the floor. "Come on, we've wasted too much time already. Me and Anna will break the door down, you two throw him in." She held up a finger. "*But*, after that, I want you both to hang back. Anna and

I will take a door each as a shield and deal with as many hunters as we can while drawing their fire, then you two come in after."

"Sounds good," I said before Michaela or Gracie could protest. I pushed myself off the wall and shoved my lingering worry to one side.

"Let's finish this."

17

We rounded the corner. The double doors to the main operations room looked innocuous enough, white, like everything else in the damned place, with little blacked out windows set near the top. Colette nudged me as we inched closer, nodding to a camera pointed right at us. I let out a rush of air. They *definitely* knew we were coming. Doubts about our plan crept through my mind, but as I didn't want to cause a panic, I kept my thoughts to myself.

Not thinking about if this was my last day on earth, not thinking about if this was Colette's last day, or Michaela's or Gracie's, or even Saira's—although I hoped she wasn't still in the building, never mind the main operations room—I caught Colette's eye, and together we burst into synchronised action, the kind of coordinated only people who knew each other inside out could achieve.

I lined up in front of the left door and used my considerable strength to knock it clean off its hinges. I ducked down and to the side with it while Michaela and Gracie threw the body in. It sailed past me, moving far more gracefully than a dead body should. It landed with a thump on laminated floor, skidding slightly before it came to an anticlimactic stop.

No one fired anything. No one made any sudden movements. I stayed crouched behind my door, my breathing heavy, wondering if I peeked out, I'd get an eyeful of dart.

The siren cut off.

My ears continued ringing, but in the sudden silence nineteen heartbeats thundered, not including my group. What kind of trap was this? Dread dripped down my spine.

"You can come out. We want to talk."

That voice plucked at my memory. Luke. What was going on?

I edged my head around the door, still holding it in front of the majority of my body. Rows of computers greeted my eyes, as well as several TV screens mounted on the far wall. It looked like any run-of-the-mill office space, with little potted plants dotted around and random artwork on the magnolia wall. We were still underground, but they even had fake windows to brighten the place up. The eighteen hunters armed and armoured to the teeth, and the seventeen guns pointed right at us, ruined the quaint little office illusion. The eighteenth gun was pointed at Saira, who stood next to Luke, still in her hoodie from earlier. Not a piece of armour in sight.

Shit.

My fangs dropped down, and I snarled at them all. If they couldn't kill us, they were going to threaten Saira to make us capitulate. *Fucking* hunters, using one of their own like that. Disgusting.

"What is going on?" I growled.

"I'd like an answer to that question myself," Luke said, grabbing Saira's arm and shaking her roughly. I'd show him rough. I'd tear him limb from limb. Fury sparked a wildfire in my bones, and each flex of his hand on her arm stoked the flames higher.

"Perhaps Saira would like to explain?" Luke continued, his other hand tightening around the grip of his gun. Abominable inventions. Humans loved thinking up new ways to kill each other. I *hated* that such a thing was pointed at Saira.

At least she looked more pissed off than scared. I took solace in that. I wouldn't want to see her terrified.

"I've already told you, I don't know," she snapped, her eyes flashing with anger. "I left the building, the strike team went in, they all came out unconscious. Maybe the strike team fucked up somewhere."

"Enough with the bullshit," Luke snarled. His grip on Saira's arm looked bruising. She must've been in pain, but none of it showed on her face. "You obviously warned them. Sam was right, wasn't she? You're in league with fucking vampires."

He shoved her away from himself, levelling the gun at her with both hands as she stumbled into a desk. I took an unconscious step forward but stopped when the other hunters responded in kind.

Luke laughed. A horrible grating sound that offended my already raw ears. "Look at her," he said, pointing his chin at me. "She's furious. It's way more than just fucking, isn't it? You two in some kind of relationship?" His lip curled in disgust, and an answering revulsion twisted my own face. I was so *sick* of homophobic arseholes. "Sam figured it out, and you killed her for it. You're a disgrace to your species." He paused, a different kind of disgust smoothing over his expression. "She turned you, didn't she?"

"What? No—"

"Don't *fucking* lie. Show me your teeth. *Now.*"

Luke took half a step towards Saira, aggression steaming from his body, and I didn't wait a second longer.

Holding the door out in front of me like a battering ram, I charged at Luke. I had the vague sense of Colette—and I think Michaela and

Gracie—doing the same with the other hunters, but I didn't turn from my dash forward.

Despite my speed, he managed to point his gun at me and get three rounds off before we barrelled into each other. The two of us went flying into the wall with the monitors, rattling them in their frames. I threw the door aside and pushed myself to my feet, baring my fangs and readying myself to tear into him.

Instead, I lurched to my left.

What the fuck? I looked down, belatedly registering pain. Two ragged holes had appeared in my body, one in my left thigh and one in my lower stomach. I ground my jaw as realisation smacked me over the head. Two of the bastard's wild shots had actually hit me. The one in my thigh had gone right though, missing bone and major arteries, but the one in my stomach was still lodged inside. The lump of metal burned, an invasion my body wouldn't tolerate, and agony spiked as it began to move.

I'd been shot only a handful of times in my life, and I much preferred the through and through ones. When bullets got stuck, when my body pushed them out, it was *excruciating*. I'd often said I wouldn't wish the pain on my worst enemy, but right then, I would. Fuck Luke for pointing a weapon at Saira and fuck him for shooting me.

I didn't have time to stop and wait for the bullet to fall out. Luke was back on his feet, gun in hand, teeth gritted. I pushed my damaged body forward, slower than normal, the pain making every nerve scream, but nothing would stop me from tearing him apart.

Saira got to him first.

She kicked the gun from his hand, and the two of them started fighting. And I mean full on brawling. I blinked in astonishment; the movies always got it wrong. It wasn't choreographed, it wasn't scripted, neither pulled their punches. I'd seen countless fist fights in my time, and they were always brutal.

I moved to help—no matter how good Saira was, and she was good, Luke was taller and stronger and outweighed her. It was only a matter of time before he gained the upper hand.

A dart grazing the air in front of my face stopped me in my tracks. All at once, I became aware of the larger fight around me.

Four of the other seventeen hunters were down, but so was Gracie. Colette still had her door and Michaela used part of a desk as a shield. They tag teamed well, but two against thirteen were not good odds. I spared a quick glance at Saira and Luke, uncertainty briefly paralysing me, but then had to duck another dart. That decided for me. I couldn't help anyone if I was unconscious.

Sending Saira all the luck in the world, I pushed my aching body towards the other hunters. Dodging twice more, rage battled the agony in my stomach. I made it about halfway across the room before I jerked to the side as another fucking bullet tore through my body. In through my back, out through my abdomen.

I saw red.

My world boiled down to senses and instinct. The room was large, but it still felt hot and crowded as people fought for their lives. Sweat pushed out of everyone's pores and the heat made my skin feel too tight over my body. The smell of blood saturated the air, exquisite in its ubiquitousness, and I had to fight my rising bloodlust. The bullet wounds didn't help. Blood helped us heal faster, so we craved it whenever injured.

Shouts and grunts made for an awful music, the melody jarring and unpleasant. I wanted to silence them all.

So that's what I did.

I tore into the nearest hunter, his back to me as he focused on Michaela. I allowed myself a single, glorious gulp of blood before I picked up his dying body and threw it at two others. I followed quickly, throwing a computer at another hunter who attempted to aim at me. Of the two I'd knocked down with the third, only one had regained his feet. I stomped on the neck of the one still scrambling around on the ground and swatted the gun out of the other one's hand. Relishing the wide-eyed look of horror he gave me, I descended on him and tore out his throat.

The next few minutes passed in the same manner. Duck or dodge a dart, tear into a hunter, revel in their blood. Their superior numbers couldn't match my ferocity, and I cut through them with almost clinical precision. My earlier thoughts of hunters growing fat and lazy turned out to be true; in this current day and age, they were used to sneaking up on us and rendering us unconscious from afar. They weren't prepared for three awake and aware vampires fighting back. It was pathetic, really.

I remembered one particular hunter, from what was then the Holy Roman Empire, doing more damage with a katzbalger than these modern hunters could with guns. That old bastard had convinced himself he was doing God's work, killing as many vampires as he could, and fanaticism was one powerful drug. It had taken five of us to eventually kill him.

These hunters in their modern armour with their modern weapons didn't hold a candle to that old hunter's zeal. I used that to my advantage.

Blood drenched me from head to foot by the time everything was over. Colette killed the last hunter, and I stood surrounded by bodies and blood, breathing hard but still breathing. Still conscious. The bullet in my stomach finally pushed its way out, and I heard a faint *clink* as it hit the floor.

That soft sound opened the floodgates on my emotions. Knee-weakening relief rushed through me, dragging along disbelief and a type of dizzying giddiness that made me clutch a desk to remain upright. We'd *won*. We'd *survived*. All we had to do was erase all the files and we'd successfully destroyed a guild. Laugher caught in my throat. It had a hysterical tint to it, but in that moment, I didn't care. This was momentous. Historic. Vampires across the world would know it was possible. Despite hunters ever advancing technology, they could still be brought down from within their very strongholds. *This day will go down in history. And I was a part of it.*

I was in shock, I know. A lot of things could've still gone wrong. Maybe re-enforcements were on their way. Maybe we wouldn't be able to delete the files. Maybe there was an army waiting outside. Maybe, maybe, maybe. I couldn't live my life on maybes. I'd take the impossible success and almost overwhelming happiness and worry about everything else later.

Michaela looked to be in as much shock as I was. She'd had as much blood covering her as I did too, and she shot me an astonished grin when she caught my eye.

Colette was... frowning at something past my shoulder. Spinning on my heel, reality shoved shock out of my head.

"Don't—"

"Shut the fuck up," Luke snarled.

I moved towards him the same moment he moved towards the door. If he thought he could escape, he was in for a rude awakening. A deafening gunshot rang out and I flinched despite myself. Except, I was fine. The idiot missed. I let out a savage yell and sped up, only to be pulled short by Colette's call.

I don't remember moving. One moment I was chasing Luke, the next I was kneeling next to Saira, pressing my hand into the bullet wound in her stomach. My mind was numb. Centuries of experience gone when confronted with Saira's blood on my hands.

"Could we get her to a hospital?" Michaela's voice was distant, distorted, and the small part of my mind still functioning dismissed her suggestion. I knew, *knew*, she'd lost too much blood. It soaked my legs. The smell of it was suffocating instead of beautiful.

I didn't hear what Colette said in answer, if she said anything at all. My eyes were caught on Saira's, and I witnessed the exact moment she saw the truth reflected in my face. She gave me a small smile even as blood trickled from her mouth.

"A-Anna," she muttered, clearly using a lot of strength just to talk. "Tell my parents... I'm sorry... I didn't come home... this time."

My eyes burned, my throat burned, fury burned in my chest. It couldn't be the end. We were just getting started. I wanted to scream and rage at the unfairness of it all, but I was frozen, my hand still pressing down even though it wasn't making any difference. Tears blurred my vision, and I blinked them away, not wanting to miss anything. Was there something I was missing? I couldn't sit and watch her die. I couldn't...

Her blood congealed against my legs, oozed passed my fingers. What could I do? What could I do? She was fading in front of me, and I remained a statue, unable to *fucking* think—

Blood. It helped heal us. My own stomach wound was already closed. My mind, frozen not a second ago, raced with possibility. But we didn't have time. If I was going to do it, it had to be *now*.

"Saira. Saira, look at me." I waited until I had her attention, hazy though it was, before continuing. "There is a way to save you, but I need your explicit consent. I won't do it if I don't have it, okay?"

Colette made a sound like surprise behind me, but I ignored it, all my focus on Saira.

"What?" she asked, her voice fainter than it had been mere seconds ago.

"I can turn you into a vampire, and you'll heal from your wounds. But I need you to give me permission."

I held my breath. I had an inkling of how difficult such a decision would be for her, but at the same time, she couldn't really give it the thought it deserved. Hesitation rippled across her face, her thoughts no doubt in chaos. But she *didn't have time*.

"Saira..." I didn't want to influence her in any way. It was her decision alone, but I needed her answer.

She nodded, a tear leaking free as she scrunched her eyes closed. "Yes. I don't... want to die."

I didn't delay. My movements were smooth and succinct as I bit down on my arm, my blood surging up as if it knew time was short. I watched as my blood dripped into her mouth, watched as she swallowed and sighed, like it was medicine.

What happened next would haunt my dreams.

18

I'd only seen one turning in my entire five centuries—not including my own—and I hadn't liked it. His name had been Janusz, a Polish man who hadn't seen a decade as a vampire. I remembered convulsions, eyes rolling back, the tendons in his neck so taut I thought they would snap. The seizure lasted a few minutes; the following unconsciousness a few hours. We hadn't been able to wake him. He'd been so still, so cold, I'd thought he'd died. All I remembered from my own turning was a brief feeling of falling.

Seeing Saira's eyes roll back as she started to convulse was not an image I would forget in a hurry. Placing my hands under her head to protect it from the hard floor, I could only watch as her body flailed out of control. It was horrible. Helplessness swept over me in a flood. Was this the best decision for her? Would she hate what she'd become? I ground my jaw and held her head and felt truly out of my depth for the first time in a long time.

When it all eventually stopped, the constraints around my chest loosened, and my lungs could finally expand again. I removed my hands as carefully as possible, stood, and stretched. It was a waiting game now. She would be unconscious for a while.

My body was whole again. No bullet holes, no tears or scratches or scars. My stomach rumbled, loud in the quiet, and Colette looked up from where she'd been glued to a computer. She gestured at the broken bodies of the hunters. "Get them while they're still warm. You've used a lot of energy. How many times were you shot?"

"Three," I mumbled, stumbling over to the nearest body. It had been A Day, both physically and emotionally, and it was probably only mid-afternoon.

Colette smirked. "So now that's six more times than me."

I paused in my feeding to let out a bark of a laugh. "I'd forgotten we were keeping score. Damn. I can't believe I'm losing."

Michaela looked over from where she was trying to wake Gracie. "You guys are tallying up how often you get shot?"

"Yep."

"That's so weird."

Colette snorted. "It was something born out of the need to distract ourselves from the pain of it. Hunters used to shoot us to slow us down centuries ago. It doesn't happen often now. I was last shot in World War Two, but that had nothing to do with vampirism and everything to do with shitty nazi's killing members of the French resistance." She grinned, showing off her fangs. "I gutted them all."

Michaela matched her savage smile. "You'll have to tell me more about it. And about what adventures you two have been on." She pointed at me, and I nodded. Michaela was almost as hungry for tales of the past as she was for blood.

She turned back to Gracie, and I moved to Colette after feeding some more. "Can we delete everything?"

Colette nodded. "I think so. If I'm remembering Lili's lessons correctly, I know what to do. I can give her access too, so she can tidy up the things I miss."

"Lili is one hell of a programmer."

"And engineer. And computer scientist. And hacker." Colette smiled. "I won't take too long. We shouldn't linger here. Who knows if they're going to launch some kind of counter offensive."

I straightened from where I'd been leaning on a desk. "I'll monitor the cameras."

"Anna."

I sighed. I knew what she was going to say. "I know I swore I'd never turn anyone but... it was the only option."

Colette took my hand and squeezed. "I understand. We make difficult decisions in the heat of the moment, but I want you to know you won't be alone with the consequences. We'll stay together for the next century, yeah?" She lifted her chin at Michaela and Gracie. "With those two, and now Saira, it will be difficult. We'll help each other help them."

I nodded once, squeezing back. "I like the sound of that. Thank you."

"I'll always be there for you."

"And I you."

Colette let go of my hand. "I know. Now get out of my way and let me do this. I was always better at computers than you."

I rolled my eyes. "Keep telling yourself that."

Not wanting to distract Colette, I picked my way over the bodies and sat next to Saira. She hadn't stirred, but her breathing was even, and her wounds had begun to heal. She would wake up ravenous. I'd have to procure a meal for her. I had a feeling she would try to reject it. At first, anyway. That initial bloodlust was too great to ignore, no matter how much you railed against it.

I wasn't sat for long. Michaela managed to wake Gracie after all but drowning her in the little blood I'd left, and Colette finished with the files in record time. Maybe she was better at computers than me. I'd never admit it.

I scooped Saira up into my arms, and the five of us left the building via the garage entrance after quickly wiping as much blood from our faces as possible and throwing oversized hunters' jackets over our bloodstained clothes. The jackets where plain black, without any kind of logo, but I knew what they were. They weighed heavy on my shoulders, and I couldn't wait to get them off and burn them.

After stealing a car—my skill with vehicles eclipsed everyone else's, to my smug satisfaction—Colette directed me to the new house she and the other botanists had been staying in. I took the scenic route, of course. The entire area looked to have been evacuated, and I didn't see anyone tailing us, but one could never to too careful. I parked as far away as I could without rousing suspicion carrying Saira.

Once at the house—detached, much bigger than the one me and Michaela had been renting—I laid Saira carefully on a bed, and lay down next to her, blood be damned. I wanted to be by her side when she woke up. The others took turns showering, and the spray of the water lulled me down into the deep depths of sleep.

19

"Anna. Anna, wake up. *Anna.*"

Rough hands shook me back to consciousness. I grumbled, annoyed to be so rudely awoken. Normally, I enjoyed early mornings. There was something so satisfying about being awake earlier than the world, like getting a head start on everyone around you.

I wasn't satisfied that morning. Nor, apparently, was it morning at all, if the blackness pressing against the window was anything to go by.

"Anna?"

The voice was small, scared, and nothing like anything I'd ever heard come out of Saira's mouth before. I immediately twisted towards her, reaching out a comforting hand. She grasped it like she was dangling from a cliff and I was her only lifeline.

"What is it?" I asked, somewhat stupidly. I knew what was wrong. *A hunter becoming a vampire.* It had surely happened before, but I'd only ever heard rumours, nothing concrete. "You're hungry." A statement rather than a question, but Saira nodded regardless.

She wrapped her arms around her stomach as a loud rumble filled the room. It absolutely *wasn't* the time or place, but I had to fight a smile. She looked so bizarrely embarrassed by such a normal bodily function that it was difficult to keep my face straight.

"Come on, let's head downstairs." Maybe the others had already found someone for her. I cursed myself for not staying awake. I told myself I'd provide for her, and there I was, sleeping on the job.

"Wait." She squeezed my hand impossibly tighter. Yeah, there was that vampire strength. She hadn't had half that power when she'd been human.

As I sat back and waited for her to talk, the congealed blood covering my clothes and body, cold and sticky and wholly unappetising, made itself known, and didn't hide my grimace of disgust. An all-encompassing urge to shower raced through me, but I ignored it and focused on Saira.

She'd lifted her hoodie up and was running the hand not clutching mine over her stomach. Her smooth, unblemished stomach. You'd never guess she'd been shot, on the verge of death, her blood doing its best to fill up the space *outside* her body.

Complex emotions played across her face. Child-like wonder followed on the heels of a heart-breaking sadness. A combination that had me sitting up straighter. I'd do my best to help her with everything, but I wasn't sure it would be enough. I'd never been a hunter. I'd never been indoctrinated with their 'kill all vampires' bullshit. I really hoped she didn't hate herself. That was the last thing I wanted for her.

"I'm a... a vampire," she said, the words hesitant, a touch unbelieving, like this was all a dream. Or nightmare, depending on perspective. "I didn't die?"

"You didn't die," I confirmed. "I turned you to save you. Do you remember?" I'd received her consent at the time, but what if she didn't remember it? What kind of ramifications would that have? I'd been turned against my will, and I'd never do the same to someone else. What if—

"I remember."

Those two words made me sag with relief. "I'm sorry if you regret it," I said, running my thumb over the back of her hand, "but I had to do something."

She didn't respond, which was fine. She probably did regret it on some level. I imagined she'd go through the entire range of emotions over the next few months, or even years, as she came to terms with what had happened yesterday.

She stopped rubbing her stomach and started rubbing her jaw. "Why do my gums hurt?" she asked, the answer already reflected in her eyes.

"Drop your fangs," I said, my words quiet.

She didn't do anything for a good few minutes. I waited, giving her all the time she needed. The silence in the house was loud, but comfortable. I wanted this to be a safe space for her. *I* wanted to be a safe space for her. So, I held her hand and sat still, a solid presence by her side she could lean on if she needed to.

She dropped them. I couldn't really see—she had turned slightly away from me, like this was something she needed to do alone—but the blissful look on her face told me everything I needed to know. Freeing our fangs was such a wonderful release.

I smiled at her when she turned to me in surprise. "Good, right? Holding them away takes effort, and unfortunately there's no trick I can teach you that alleviates it, you'll just have to get used to pushing them back in."

She did just that, and I caught her look of dissatisfaction, then her contrite look at being dissatisfied. Knowing she was a vampire and seeing the evidence were two distinct things, and her fangs were *beautiful*. I didn't expect the rush of emotion I felt at seeing them. She was like me now. I didn't have to watch her age and wither away. I would get to take her to whichever countries she wanted, see her experience different cultures, watch her grow and learn and finally *see* the world. That rush settled in my chest, bright and warm and happy.

She released and returned her fangs several times before she flopped back against the headboard with a sigh. "This is going to take some getting used to."

"Yeah, it did for me as well. But I didn't have anyone. You have me and Colette and Michaela and Gracie. We're all going to look out for each other."

Our hands were still joined, and she squeezed again. "Thank you." Those two short words carried so much conviction that a lump formed in my throat.

"I won't let you go through this alone. I know it's scary, but I'll be here for you. Now and potentially forever." I grinned, hoping to lighten the heaviness of my statement. She knew I had feelings for her of course, but I didn't want to place expectations on her shoulders she perhaps couldn't or didn't want to meet.

In lieu of an answer, Saira leaned over and captured my lips with hers. The touch was soft at first, but quickly grew hot and heavy as she pushed me down and straddled me, our tongues tangling and a moan catching in my throat. She moved to lift my top up but froze, leaving me scrambling to keep up with what was going on.

She stared at the dried blood all over my skin and clothes. Her stomach rumbled again, and I gently eased her off me. The beginnings of a wild edge in her eyes cooled all arousal. She needed blood, and she needed it soon.

"C'mon," I said, standing and pulling her after me.

She didn't say a word as I led her downstairs, nor when we found Colette on the sofa reading a magazine, an unconscious man slumped next to her.

"You're finally awake." Colette smiled at us, and I was again reminded of my want to see them get along. She jerked a thumb at the man. "Since Anna fell asleep too, I went out and found him for you. Caught him selling drugs to kids. Figured he won't be missed."

Good. We'd teach her our way. There was *so much* to teach her. Excitement built in me until I was sure I'd explode from it. Running my tongue over my teeth, I reigned it in. This was quite possibly the worst time of Saira's life, and it wouldn't do to grin with exhilaration.

"Are you okay?" Colette asked, concerned.

Case in point. Saira looked like she was about to faint. "I don't think I can kill him," she said, all colour faded from her face. "I feel the need to—to drink, but I don't think I can kill him."

I didn't want this to be any more difficult for her than it already was, and the compromise was obvious. "Would you be okay if I killed him, and you drank his blood?"

It took over half a minute for Saira to nod, but she did in the end. It was no effort at all to tear open his throat. Saira all but shoved me out of the way, well and truly in the grip of the bloodlust, especially with hot, fresh blood pouring from the man. He didn't wake up, which I counted as a good thing.

She drained him in record time, essentially being the one to kill him. I didn't say that, though. Blood dripped from her fangs and chin, and I'd never seen anything so beautiful. "How are you?" I asked, determined to be as supportive as possible.

She gave a small shrug, like she didn't know what to do with her body. "I don't know." She looked at the man, a small frown creasing her forehead and her gaze somewhat vacant. "What happens now?"

"Now," Colette stood and stretched, dropping her magazine in her seat, "you two have showers while I get rid of him. In the morning, get your affairs in order. We're leaving Ireland as soon as possible."

A list of things to do ran through my head—stop renting the house, close the bank accounts, acquire new passports, on and on it went—but I didn't say any of that.

Instead, I took Saira's hand and tugged her away from the dead body. She wiped her chin, gazing down at the glistening blood like it contained a haemorrhagic virus. *This is going to be beyond difficult for her.*

"Now," I said, holding her close as we made our way back upstairs, making sure her focus was on me and not the man she'd just fed on, "it's time to start the rest of your very long life."

Acknowledgements

As always, I would like to first thank my wife. I cannot overstate the amount of love and support you give me, just as I cannot fully articulate what it means to me. Thank you for being my champion, my 'hype-woman', my everything. Your strength pushes me forward when I don't believe in myself. I love you so much.

Secondly, thank you to everyone who beta read for me. We authors can become blind to errors, despite writing the book in the first place and then reading and rereading and rereading and rereading it. Thank you for helping me improve this.

Thank you to everyone who read and reviewed ARC's. Your early support means so much to indie authors like me. Same goes to everyone who pre-ordered. Thank you all so much, it really means the world.

And to you, readers, for picking up this book and dedicating your time to it. I hope you enjoyed it! I definitely suffered from second book syndrome writing this, and I hope it turned out okay.

As I mentioned in the *We're All Monsters Here* acknowledgements, this whole idea started life as a prompt for a writing challenge and has somehow grown into a trilogy. Yep, I'll be working on the next book very soon! I really love Anna and I can't wait to tell more of her story.

Website: amymarsden.co.uk

Instagram/Threads: amymarsdenauthor

About the author

As a child, Amy loved reading and writing, so naturally she graduated with a degree in biomedical science and has worked in a microbiology laboratory ever since. Her passion is writing, however, and she turned back to it during her years at university. When she is not writing about surviving apocalypses, vampires feeding on the rich, exploring space, and conquering magic—all celebrating queer love—she can be found reading or playing games about those very things. She lives by the sea with her wife and their seventeen-year-old cat, who still runs around like a kitten.

Printed in Great Britain
by Amazon